AF229516

Bronco of 96

The Cherokee War

Patsy H. Manley

authorHOUSE®

AuthorHouse™
1663 Liberty Drive
Bloomington, IN 47403
www.authorhouse.com
Phone: 1-800-839-8640

First published by AuthorHouse   3/22/2010

ISBN: 978-1-4490-9558-1 (e)
ISBN: 978-1-4490-9556-7 (sc)
ISBN: 978-1-4490-9557-4 (hc)

Library of Congress Control Number: 2010903634

Printed in the United States of America
Bloomington, Indiana

This book is printed on acid-free paper.

DEDICATION

I dedicate this book to my husband of 40 years.

Bill has traveled with me to research and to take pictures for both of my books.
I look forward to traveling with him for research on several more books.

Special thanks to Chad Frazier for letting me use him as an important character in this book.

PREFACE

The town of Ninety Six, South Carolina, is rich in history. In 1540, the first European presence in the area was Hernando DeSoto. He marched from the Savannah River to the Cherokee towns along the Cherokee Path. Before Charles Town (now Charleston) was founded on the coast of South Carolina, commerce and trade had already established Ninety Six as a prominent stopping place along the Cherokee Path. Traders, hunters, and other explorers frequented Robert Gouedy's Trading Post.

The Cherokee Path at Charles Town ran through Ninety Six and connected many of the Cherokee territories. From Ninety Six, the path led to Fort Prince George and Keowee, the principal town of the Cherokee Lower Settlements. Both are now under the waters of Lake Keowee.

Ninety Six, the town with a number for a name and its name in its zip code, is located in the inland regions of South Carolina on the 96 mile marker of the Cherokee Path. There is one other town on the Cherokee Path, Six Mile, which has a number in its name. There are several creeks on the mile markers. Twelve Mile Creek and Eighteen Mile Creek are located near York, South Carolina. Twenty Creek, Three and Twenty Creek, and Six and Twenty Creek are located between Anderson, SC, and Clemson University.

There are many interesting historical facts about this small rural town and its importance in the development of our state and of our country. Join Bronco as he travels the Cherokee Path and finds love and friendship along the way.

CHAPTER 1

It is July 4, 2009, in the small rural town of 96, South Carolina. The 96 Mill Village Organization and the town council have organized an all day festival, "Festival of the Stars." The opening event is a town parade. A local motorcycle club leads a number of 4-wheelers, bicycles, and several decorated tricycles. Classic cars and golf carts follow the vehicles.

Leading the second wave of the parade is a group of teenage boys dressed as Indians. The tallest boy wears a buckskin outfit and war paint. His name is Bronco Manley. He has lived in 96 all of his life. His best friend Michael is wearing only a breech cloth and moccasins. Not only does he have war paint on his face, but on his arms, legs, and chest.

"Michael," Bronco whispers. "There's Kristin and Kathy. Let's see if we can scare them. You go left and I'll go right."

"Yeah!" Michael snickers. "We'll sneak up behind them and let out some war whoops."

The mischievous boys come up quietly behind the girls. They whoop and holler as loud as they can. The girls scream and run for their lives. Michael is laughing so hard he can't stand up.

"Michael, get up off the ground! The girls are getting away." Bronco reaches out to help Michael. "Come on. You can finish laughing later. Right now we need to get back to the parade. I hope my mom and dad didn't see us fooling around. They get so jacked out of shape every time I try to have some fun."

Bronco and Michael meander through the crowd until they reach their section of the parade. Bronco wipes his forehead and sighs deeply, "Well, I think we just might get away with it this time."

As the girls slow down and catch their breath, Kristin vows, "They are not going to get away with this. They almost made me wet my pants. We have to do something to pay them back."

"I agree," Kathy is breathing hard, "but it has to be something drastic. We'll just butter them up until the right opportunity comes along. Then we'll stick it to them *real* good."

The parade pulls into the town park where games, rides, and old-fashioned contests are in progress. The mayor begins the festival with a short speech. "We are happy to have all of you with us to celebrate the 4th of July. We are sad our nation is in the midst of the War for Iraqi Freedom, but I'm sure our soldiers want us to continue festivals and firework displays to commemorate the war fought for our independence, The Revolutionary War."

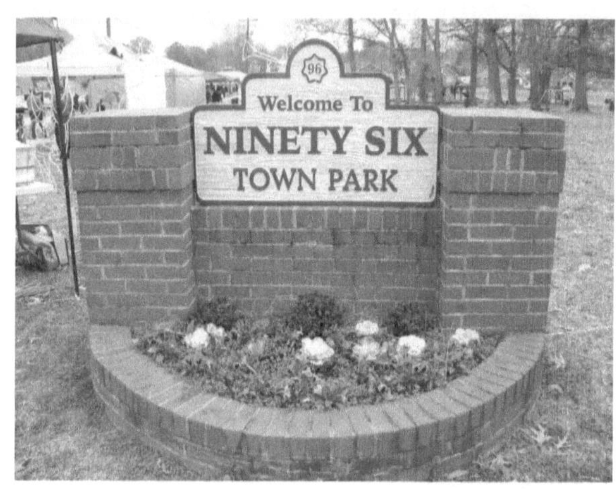

The mayor continues, "Due to the state of the economy, many festivals have been dropped. Greenwood is no different. For over 20 years, our technical college has provided games, rides, and fireworks for the enjoyment of the surrounding area. Due to educational cutbacks by the state, it was announced in May that the festival would no longer be sponsored by the college."

The mayor pauses, "I am proud to say that the internet news site known as Greenwood Today originated in 96. After the announcement, Greenwood Today's staff began a campaign to raise $10,000 so our town could sponsor a fireworks display. They challenged individuals to donate $96 toward a town celebration. Greenwood Today, the 96 Mill Village Association, and 96 citizens raised the necessary funds in less than two months. Congratulations, it is *you* who have pulled together this festival and fireworks display. By the power invested in me, I proclaim this to be the 'First Annual Festival of the Stars'."

Deafening applause and hip-hip-hoorays explode over the park. People are shaking hands and hugging necks. The citizens of 96 are indeed proud of what they've accomplished.

Michael turns to Bronco. "Can you believe how silly these grown-ups are acting? I'm glad my mom's not here today. I would be embarrassed."

Bronco laughs, "I didn't have any choice. You know my mom and dad come to everything. You couldn't keep them away. I just do my best to avoid being seen with them."

"Yeah, but that's hard to do. They'll be tracking you down so they can show you off to people they haven't seen in a long time. Don't you just hate it when they treat you like a new puppy? They pat you on the back and then rub your head. Their friends say how cute you are and how much you look like your mom or dad. Then, they tell you to go play in the park. "

"You are *so-o-o* right, Michael. Festivals are for old people. Just look at the silly rides. And if the merry-go-round, train rides and live pony rides aren't embarrassing enough, we have games such as bean-bag-toss, go fishing and picking up ducks. Geez, they must think we are still children. They could at least have a roller coaster or a bullet for us to ride."

Bronco adds, "Consider this. We have music, but it's all a throwback to our parent's childhood, not ours. Now I ask you. Have you ever heard of *Hack Bartley and Shuffle*? He must be ancient. His hair is as white as my dad's. In fact, my folks went to high school with him. They say he was a member of the 'great' singing group known as the *Swinging Medallions*. Man, all this beach music is for the seagulls, not for me." The boys laugh. "Next year they'll probably have a country music group. Why don't they ask us who we would like to have?"

"Because they're doing all this for themselves," Michael repeats. "They are reliving their youth. I wish they'd give us a chance to live our youth instead of theirs."

"Well, I tell you what," Bronco leans toward Michael. "I'm not sticking around here and grow old like my parents. Let's go find some fun."

The music starts on the stage. *Hack Bartley and Shuffle* begin the festivities. "Folks, we've been asked to start the fun with something different. Two locals have volunteered to come on stage and perform with us."

Hack pauses. "Bronco Manley and Michael Bell, where are you? Come up on stage."

Kristin and Kathy walk up behind the stunned boys and push them toward the stage.

Michael's eyes open wide. "What's going on here?"

Kathy's sweet little smile shows him that the girls are behind whatever is about to happen.

"I think you'll enjoy what we've planned for you and Bronco."

Kristin giggles. "You guys didn't

really think we'd let you get away with what you did. You embarrassed us, and Uncle Hack is helping us with our payback. Now, get on that stage!"

Bronco and Michael have no choice. They climb up on the stage where the executioner waits.

Kristen laughs. "Nothing is sweeter than revenge served cold."

Kathy has a serious look on her face. "Who said that?"

"I don't remember. I don't pay a lot of attention in my Shakespeare class, but I'm definitely going to enjoy this."

"Here's my guys, now. I understand you are two of our biggest fans in 96 and your favorite song dates back to my days with the *Swinging Medallions*. We are happy you want to dance with us to the classic 'Doubleshot of My Baby's Love'."

Looking first to his band, Hack winks. "What do you guys say?" He pauses and then turns to the crowd. "What do you citizens of 96 say about this?"

The crowd roars as the band begins the familiar chords of the classic hit. Hack shows Bronco and Michael the basic dance step. He places Bronco on one side of the band and Michael on the other.

Hack motions to the guys. "Use the step I just showed you and then follow the band members for the rest."

It doesn't take long for Bronco and Michael to catch the rhythm and attempt to out dance the band members.

The song ends. "Guys, you were fantastic!! What do you 96'ers think of their performance?"

The crowd roars while applauding and jumping into the air.

"Guys, you were awesome! You two fit right in with the band. Are you interested in joining us on tour as dancers?" Hack laughs as he applauds the good sports. "Take a bow, guys!"

The crowd encourages Bronco and Michael who take bows and even throw kisses to their adoring fans. They jump from the stage and find the girls on the front row.

Bronco speaks first, "That was great! Thanks for getting us this gig! We haven't had this much fun in a long, long time. Right, Michael?" The boys are still flushed and breathless from the experience.

The girls are stunned. Kristin speaks up. "Bronco, we didn't want you to like it. We wanted payback. You and Michael were supposed to be embarrassed and miserable. You just ruined everything." The girls stomp away.

"What did we do?" Bronco and Michael call after them. "Why're you so mad at us? We didn't do anything wrong. We were just having a good time."

Michael laughs and cuts his eyes at Bronco. "We really turned the table on them, didn't we? High 5! We are still the payback kings!"

Laughingly Bronco says, "You know the girls are still mad at us about this morning, don't you? They definitely feel the need to punish us. I think we had better watch them closely. They're not finished with us, yet."

"You're right. I say we come up with something else before they do." Michael thinks for a minute. "I know we can talk them into going closer to the fireworks exhibit. We won't tell them where they are. Then, the noise and the lights will scare them, but we'll be there to rescue them with hugs and kisses. Ha! Ha! It'll be great."

"Yeah! Huh! You don't really think they're going to hug and kiss us while the fireworks go off. Get real, Michael. Our girls aren't that gullible, but I would like to go up to the complex and look around. The area is roped off, and you know what that means. It's like an open invitation to 'come on down.' I'd like to see what the fireworks setup looks like before it goes off."

"OK! Let's go exploring." Then Michael challenges, "I bet I can beat you to the complex."

"And I'll just take that bet. You've never beaten me in a foot race. See you when you get there, slow poke."

"It's true. Michael has never outrun Bronco. This time is no exception. Bronco arrives at the complex with time to spare. The area is roped off and has signs about the danger of explosions.

A typical teenager, Bronco doesn't hesitate to crawl under the yellow warning tape. As he turns to give Michael his victory jump, a freak event occurs. Some premature explosions push Bronco toward a huge white light. He feels himself being pulled into a vortex for the second time in less than a month.

"Oh, no! This can't be happening again. I must be the unluckiest person in 96. I hope I get back in time for graduation."

CHAPTER 2

The bright light grows larger and larger until it finally bursts. It is exactly like the explosion at the stockade-fort that ended his first leap into the past.

"Oh, no!" Bronco yells. He is back in Old 96. Once again he sees the storage building as it explodes. He throws himself onto the ground and covers his head. The force of the blast blows away the backside of the building that doubles as a part of the outer wall.

He lifts his head. He sees his dad and the other men lying on the ground with their heads covered. No one is hurt.

"Dad," Bronco calls. "Are you OK? Is anyone hurt?" Bronco walks into the shed to examine what is left. "We had rifles and supplies in here. The gunpowder alone should've made an explosion that could be seen for miles. We should be dead, or at least hurt. There should be debris everywhere. The explosion should have been much greater."

Bronco's dad, William, follows him into the shed. "There are no weapons or gunpowder left in this shed. This wall was rigged to blow as a distraction. The charge was ignited by a rifle from a distance. Someone planned this so we wouldn't realize our guns and ammo were gone. Who do you think could have done this?"

"It had to be Shad. It's my fault, Dad. He was invited in because of me. He came into the village to rob us of our supplies. He used me as means to an end. I'll go after him and bring back what he has stolen. I'll leave at first light."

"You can't go alone, son. You'll need some help. I'll go with you."

"Dad, I would rather you didn't. I'll take Michael and Jonathan with me. I can use them to send messages to you, but I'll take care of Shad myself."

"Son, I'm disappointed you don't want me to go; but, at least you're taking the terrible two-some with you. They'll keep you busy, if not entertained."

Daylight brings rain and fog. It's difficult to find the trail.

Michael interrupts Bronco's thoughts. "How can you tell which way they went? I don't see anything."

Bronco speaks sharply, "Michael, I'll do the tracking. You do the carrying." Then he stops what he's doing. "I'm sorry. Just let me think about this and I'll explain it to you. Deal?"

"Deal. I'll just talk to Jonathan so you can think by yourself."

Bronco laughs loudly, "You haven't changed a bit, have you? Always the clown."

Bronco looks at Jonathan, "Are you ready to have Michael speak only to you?"

Jonathan laughs, "Oh, no! My ears will be bleeding before we're five miles away from town."

These few minutes of male bonding start the trip on a good note. Bronco relaxes and enjoys the company of his two young friends.

"These tracks probably belong to Shad. He and his friends must have made several trips to the fort for the guns and ammo. Once they had all of our supplies, they made carriers of strong limbs and hides. Two people can easily carry supplies by placing the ends of the limbs on their shoulders. A group of Indians can move quickly with evenly distributed loads."

"Why didn't they bring horses and wagons?"

"Michael, only a white man would ask a question like that. Horses and wagons aren't only noisy, but they're slow. Look at this trail. A wagon can't navigate here. Warriors can."

Bronco smiles, "Since I'm responsible for you missing school today, I'll take care of your lessons. Now pay attention and learn some important things. We're going to Keowee. It's a major Cherokee town and the starting point of this path."

Michael interrupts. "Is it 96 miles from here? Does it have anything to do with the name of our town?"

Bronco explains, "We are located on the 96 mile marker of this trail."

Jonathan laughs loudly, "I often wondered about our name. I thought we were named after Mr. Gouedy because he's 96 years old."

Michael joins in on the fun. "I knew Mr. Gouedy was old, but I didn't think he was that old. Besides, I never thought the town was named after him. I thought someone was counting towns as they walked here from Charles Town, and we were the 96th town from the coast."

They all laugh.

"Golly! Gee!" Bronco exclaims. "I don't know what to think about you two boys. But I'll pass your theories on to my mom. She'll really get a hoot out of them."

Jonathan laughs, "Now that I think about it, I've always had trouble keeping Mr. Gouedy and Mr. Brown straight. Since Mr. Brown runs a store and Mr. Gouedy runs a trading post, I thought they were brothers who split one business."

"Come on, guys. You're really reaching way out to top one another's stories. This is *not* one of your sleepovers where each guy tries to tell a better story than the others."

Michael leans close to Jonathan and whispers, "Wouldn't you just love to pick up a rock and throw it at Bronco?"

"I heard that Michael. Be careful. I might be the one throwing rocks."

CHAPTER 3

It is sunset and time for some rest.

"I hear water nearby. Michael, you and Jonathan take the canteens and fill them. I'll build a small fire pit. The group should be far ahead, but we'll still be careful. Shad could be hanging back to stop us."

Michael is confused. "Bronco, you give Shad a lot of credit. Do you think he's clever enough to stop us?"

"Shad did several things that make me wary of him. First, he knew how to read my plans for building the stockade-fort. Second, he worked side by side with our men cutting down trees. Third, he helped in storing the supplies in the building. He removed the supplies from under our noses, and then blew up the shed to cover his escape. He's most definitely an intelligent man with an ulterior motive. It's probably his job to hang back and keep us from overtaking his group and regaining our supplies. Be on the lookout for obstacles, traps, and anything out of the ordinary. Never underestimate your opponent."

"I thought Indians weren't smart," Jonathan states. "After all, they live in huts, not houses."

Michael changes the subject, "Bronco, I know Shad isn't Cherokee. What is he?"

"I'm not sure. I met him only once for just a few minutes. Now, go fill our canteens."

Bronco builds a small fire pit. He opens the bag his mom packed for him. Her famous deer jerky is on the top. She has included a bag of spices for his soup, and coffee and tea for his comfort. She added some radishes, corn meal, dried beans, flour, dried tomatoes, and some potatoes for roasting or boiling.

"Mom," Bronco speaks aloud, "you always know what to pack. Let me see if you included the most important item. Oh, yes. There they are. The much needed special wipes for taking care of business. You spend so much time drying the shucks from the corn and pressing them into sheets. Then you put something on them that smells good. Sometimes you put messages on the sheets. My friends at school always enjoyed your little sayings. Oh, there it is! 'A son is a blessing counted.' We should patent your toilet leaves and make a fortune selling them to others."

He hears Michael and Jonathan racing through the woods. They are yelling and laughing.

"Bronco, come with us to the river. You won't believe what we found."

"Calm down, boys. I just finished telling you we need to be careful. Shad and his friends could be close enough to hear you. Then our journey would be useless."

"But Bronco," Jonathan giggles, "we found gold. We're going to be rich."

"Just a minute, boys. There's no gold here. It's been checked out many times by many people. I'll check out what you have found in the morning. Now, we must rest. My mom sent us some deer jerky. It'll have to do for tonight. Perhaps tomorrow we'll find something to satisfy our appetites a little more. Now, go to sleep."

The young men can't sleep. They are excited about what they've found.

"Boys, stop talking. I need my rest. Now, go to sleep, please."

The boys don't sleep, but they stop talking. They know how far to push Bronco, and they were at that point.

The next morning is cold and damp when the boys show Bronco their find.

He explains, "I'm sorry, guys. This is only placer gold. The real lode could be nearby, or it could be miles from here. Placer gold is eroded from the veins of ore deposits and makes its way into rivers and streams like this one. It gets caught in cracks and crevices of the river bedrock. It would take a great deal of time and effort to pan enough gold from this river to make it worthwhile. When you grow up, you can return to this spot and start your career as gold prospectors."

He pauses, "But for now, we will **not** search for gold. We'll continue our search for what is ours. The guns and powder that were stolen are as valuable as any gold you might find here. So, let's get on the move."

The boys sulk but don't complain. They follow Bronco back to the path and continue the journey.

CHAPTER 4

The trio travel quietly. They stop several times to rest and snack on deer jerky.

"Well, guys. By tomorrow afternoon we should be at Long Cane River. Some French Huguenots have a settlement there."

Michael whispers to Jonathan, "Do you think there might be some girls our age there? That's the bad thing about 96. There aren't any girls our age."

"Don't let Bronco hear you. Since Mary broke his heart, he hasn't talked to a girl. I feel sorry for him."

"Jonathan, did I hear you say you felt sorry for me?"

"Well, yeah. I feel sorry for you having to put up with the two of us."

"I don't believe that, but I'll accept it. It looks like a storm is close. Let's find some trees for hanging the tarp. We'll make us a shelter. It's going to be a hard rain. We'd better dig a trench around our shelter so the rain will run off. We'll have to sleep propped against the trees, but at least we'll be dry."

Amazingly, Jonathan and Michael find the perfect trees for the shelter. Some strong, low branches support the tarp and even allow them enough room to lie down.

The storm arrives just as they crawl under the shelter. Despite the thunder and the sound of the rain hitting the tarp, all three fall asleep quickly. When they awake the following morning, they find the surrounding earth wet. But, they are dry.

"OK, boys. Have some jerky for breakfast. By the time we finish this trip, you'll be so tired of deer jerky you won't hunt deer for a long time. In fact, you'll turn and run as soon as you see one coming."

Michael and Jonathan laugh. Michael says, "I love deer jerky, so I hope you're wrong."

It's Bronco's time to laugh. "On the first long trip with my dad, we ate so much deer jerky that I hated it for years. You may hate deer jerky, too, after this trip."

"Watch your steps, guys. The ground is muddy and slippery."

Late in the afternoon they reach Long Cane Creek.

Bronco yells, "The last one in is a rotten egg." They run into the water to cool off.

It isn't long until a water fight breaks out. Bronco climbs up the bank to watch the display of immaturity.

"Play time's over. We'll follow the creek north to its source. Perhaps there'll be some girls your age at the settlement."

Then, with a sad face, Bronco says, "I'm sure I won't find any women my age. After all, the women my age are old, and they're either married or just plain ugly."

The boys' mouths drop open and their eyes bulge. They look at each other, and then look at Bronco who is laughing loudly.

"Thanks, guys. That reaction was priceless. I needed a good laugh."

The boys follow in disbelief. How does he know what they talked about? Could he read their minds? The trip north becomes a silent one.

Late in the afternoon, the group approaches Long Cane Settlement.

"Look at the houses," Michael is jumping up and down with joy. "These people have a regular town, not just a settlement."

Jonathan adds, "The Indians are closer to them than to us. Do you think they're aware of the Indian problem?"

"I don't know, but I'll inform the leader. Are you feeling lucky, guys? Food, not girls." Bronco is enjoying all this.

The leader of the settlement comes to meet them. "Welcome to our village. I'm Pierre Garcon. Come. Join us for our evening meal."

"Thank you, Pierre. My friends and I will be happy to join you."

The meal is very simple. The women boil a small rabbit, add a few dried vegetables, and stir in some flour to thicken the broth.

Michael motions to Jonathan, "Look over next to that tall tree. She's looking at me. I'm going over and talk to her."

"Michael, do you think every girl in the world is interested in you?"

"Of course I do," Michael stands as tall as he can. "I haven't met a girl yet who could resist my charms."

"You are so conceited."

"No, I'm not," Michael confidently states. "Conceit is a fault, and I'm perfect."

Jonathan watches Michael saunter over to the young lady. A few minutes later, Michael offers his arm, and they walk to the banquet area of the village.

CHAPTER 5

Bronco pats Jonathan on the shoulder. "Some day you, too, will be a charming young man. You're what we refer to as a 'late bloomer.' Be patient. Let's enjoy some good food and good fellowship with our new friends."

The meal is outstanding. Once again Bronco is amazed at what frontier women can accomplish with minimal supplies. Linen tablecloths, real beverage glasses, and wildflowers in crystal vases are placed on each table in the community banquet area.

Bronco sits next to Pierre. "Your group has made great progress. Hard work and creativity is apparent. You have built a new life, but not at the expense of your traditions. How did you come to settle here?"

"In France, we owned land. Trouble grew between the Catholics and the Protestants until the Queen Mother ordered our deaths. 20,000 French Huguenots were murdered in Paris because of their Protestant faith."

Bronco is shocked. Pierre continues, "First, we came to Pennsylvania, but it wasn't what we were looking for. Then the Cherokee gave up this land between Long Cane Creek and 96. When the Indians signed the 'Rights of Occupancy,' we came here."

Pierre smiles and nods his head, "Enough about us, I've heard many good things about your village of 96. Tell me, why is it named 96?"

Bronco laughs loudly. "You aren't the first person to ask that question. The answer is simple. We are located on the 96 mile marker of the Cherokee Trail that goes all the way from the main Cherokee village to Charles Town. The Indians established this path long before the pilgrims landed at Plymouth Rock. Over the years, many trading posts have popped up along the trail."

"You're right. The answer really is simple. The spot is a mile marker on a trade route. But, what is it 96 miles from?"

They laugh together. "It's 96 miles from Keowee, the largest Cherokee Village in this area."

The conversation is now very relaxed.

"My friend, we have several talented musicians in our colony who would like to share some sounds of our homeland with you. Enjoy some food and drink while you enjoy the music. My people will prepare a nice, comfortable place for you to sleep tonight."

The music is both comforting and pleasing. Michael and Jonathan are seated with several young ladies at a long table.

Bronco overhears Michael, "This is the best meal I've had since I left 96. I love deer jerky, but give me a break. This bread and stew is great. Did you help prepare it?"

The young lady whispers, "I killed the rabbit that's in the stew. I'd rather hunt than cook. My dad tells my mom I'll outgrow the hunting stage, and then she can teach me how to be a girl."

"I love to hunt, too. But I must say, you add new meaning to the words 'buckskin pants.' Back home in 96, the girls wear dresses and walk around like they are queens of the world. You, I can talk to."

Renee smiles, "Michael, what are you doing out here in the wilderness?"

"Bronco is like my big brother. A guy stole our supplies and ammunition from our fort. We're going to find him and take our supplies back. Bronco says the thief lives with the Cherokee at Keowee."

"Bronco is so lucky to have someone like you to take care of him," Renee's eyes twinkle. "Is Jonathan your brother?"

"No, he's just a good friend. Bronco lets him tag along with us. He gathers the wood for the fire and does other small jobs."

"Oh, you mean he's everybody's little brother, huh?"

"That's right. Hey, would you like to go for a walk?"

"Yes, I would," Renee giggles and takes Michael's hand. "There is a waterfall a short distance from here. Would you like to see it?"

"Yes, I would. I'm fascinated by waterfalls." The couple walks along a secluded path leading away from the village.

Jonathan hears Michael and Renee's conversation. He mumbles to himself as he follows them through the forest. "Yeah, and I'll spy on you like a good little brother and watch for a chance to bug you."

Michael exclaims. "I can see why you like coming here! The falls are beautiful! Is that a path leading to the top?"

Renee nods yes, but adds, "The path is too slippery to climb all the way to the top. Father says it's too dangerous, so no one is allowed to go to the top."

Michael brags, "I can make it to the top. I'm like a spider climbing a wall. Watch this."

The climb to the half-way point is easy. Then the rocks become slippery. Michael grabs for a limb on a nearby bush. His foot slips, and he falls into the waters that cascade down the rocks to the pond beneath.

Jonathan hears Renee scream. He races along the path. He sees Michael tumbling down the rocks. He dives headlong into the pond and brings Michael to the surface. By the time he reaches the shoreline, Bronco and Pierre are there to pull both boys from the water.

Bronco forces air into Michael's lungs, "Michael, wake up. Breathe."

Michael draws a deep breath and screams, "My leg. My leg. I think it's broken."

They carry Michael back to the village where the doctor sets the broken leg. "This young man is very lucky. He has a clean break, but he shouldn't be moved for at least a week."

Pierre speaks up. "Michael is welcome to stay with us. You can send for him when you have finished your business."

Bronco is relieved. He needs to find Shad and the supplies. "Are you sure about taking on this responsibility?"

"Yes, I'm sure. Renee will take very good care of him until you return."

"Jonathan and I will leave at sunrise. Thank you for your help. Please explain to Michael we'll come back for him as soon as possible."

CHAPTER 6

Sunrise reveals two lone travelers on a well used path. The taller of the two watches for the signs of previous travelers who are carrying a heavy load.

"Jonathan, look at this. The rain hasn't washed away the deepest footprints. It's possible they are dropping their guard. We might have the element of surprise."

Jonathan's words become more excited, "Look! Is that a mountain?"

"Yes, it's beautiful. We sound like a couple of small children, don't we? I'm 25 years old, a full grown man, and this is the first time I've seen a mountain range." He pauses as they look at the mountains. "I was born in Ireland, and we came to America when I was two years old. I've heard my mom and dad talk about the mountains back home, but I don't remember them. The only places I remember are Charles Town and 96. I hear the Cherokee village is in the heart of the mountains."

Jonathan breaks the spell as he asks, "How much farther? It seems like we've been traveling forever."

"We aren't half way, yet. I would guess one or two more days. According to Mr. Gouedy, we should be at the healing springs tomorrow. He says the hot, mineral springs sooth the body and heal the soul. I think we could both use a bath in healing waters."

Jonathan laughs, "You certainly need a bath, Bronco. I've been behind you since we left 96. But, if you insist, I'll be glad to bathe, too. Who knows? We might find some nice young girls up the trail."

Bronco laughs as he fakes a back fist at the little smart-alec kid. "Jonathan, you aren't old enough to shave, and here you're talking about romancing girls. Michael really lucked up at the Long Cane village. Do you think he might've broken his leg so he could stay there with that little filly?"

"I know we're joking and laughing at Michael's expense, but I wouldn't put anything past him. Besides, he likes to be the center of attention. I bet he has that little girl jumping with every command he issues."

"Listen, I hear a river up ahead. It should be the Rocky River."

Jonathan grins, "I bet I know why it's called the Rocky River." He laughs at his own joke. "And, I don't need to take any guesses. Let's catch some fish for our supper. I'm tired of pemmican."

"You know, my dad used to joke about the different ways to eat pemmican. He said the best thing to do is boil it to make a stew. First, you find a horseshoe you don't need. Then, you toss it in the water with the pemmican. When the horseshoe is soft and tender, dip out the pemmican and throw it away. Add some onions, potatoes and spices to the broth, and you'll have a delicious stew."

Jonathan hiccups. "Now, I'm even more desperate for fish tonight."

A few hours later, Bronco finds a good fishing spot. "Look at this V-shaped rock pattern in the creek. Come over here and I'll show you the Indian way to catch a fish. First, the Indians build a trap by placing rocks in a V-shaped pattern. The fish swim into it and are unable to find a way out of the trap. The young braves reach under a big rock like this one. They set a finger like a hook.

When the fish latch onto the finger, they pull the fish from under the rock. Now, isn't that simple?"

"I'm not fishing that way. I like using a cane pole and a worm. I'll wait until I find a pole. Until then, I'll just watch you catch a couple of fish before I try."

"Well, here comes the first one. Catch it! It's your supper." He tosses the fish to Jonathan. "Now, I'll catch mine."

"And I'll gather some firewood."

"Oh, no, you won't. I'm not real sure how close we are to Shad and his friends. We can't risk having a fire."

"Then how will we cook our fish?"

"Have you ever heard of sushi? In China, they don't cook fish. They eat it raw."

"Bronco, stop kidding. I can't eat raw fish. You're just fooling with me."

"No, I'm not. However, I do remove the scales before I eat. Aah, come on, Jonathan. Try one little bite." Bronco takes a piece of the fish and tries to place it in Jonathan's mouth. "Here comes the sushi. Open your mouth, and it'll swim right in."

"You can treat me like a baby, but I'm still not going to eat raw fish."

"'Then, go hungry," Bronco laughs. "I'll eat both."

CHAPTER 7

Jonathan's stomach growls and moans all night. Hunger keeps him awake. He knows Bronco will have a great time ribbing him tomorrow. He is correct.

"Come on, Jonathan. Keep up. You walk like you didn't have anything to eat last night," Bronco tries to stifle his laughter but finally gives in and laughs heartily. "I hope you learned a lesson from all this."

"Exactly what lesson might that be?"

"Well, for one thing, you could learn to eat a variety of foods." He pauses to laugh. "Also, your stomach is roaring loud enough for Shad and his friends to locate us."

"Ah, come on. It's not roaring that loud."

Bronco corrects him, "Oh, yes, it is. Walk up here in front of me and scare off all the dangerous animals."

Jonathan is unable to laugh it off, so he walks in front of Bronco. Suddenly, his ankle twists, but he doesn't fall down. A rope has been placed to the side of the rock. He steps in a loop that grabs his ankle. The trap was meant for Bronco. Jonathan is almost weightless in comparison, so the rope throws him high into the air and slams him into a tree.

"Jonathan, lie still. Don't move. Let me check you out." Bronco feels Jonathon's arms and legs. Nothing is broken. "OK. Listen to me. I'll help you walk. We aren't far from the Due West Trading Post. There will be someone there who can check you for injuries. Stay awake, man. You hit your head. You might have a concussion. Stay awake."

Bronco travels as fast as he can. They arrive at the trading post a few hours later.

"Please, sir. Is there a doctor nearby?"

"We have someone trained with herbs and spices. I'll send for him. He might be able to help you. Put the boy back here in my storage room. There's a small cot where he can rest. I'll get you some water and food. You both look like you could use a hot bath and a hot meal."

"Yes, sir. We need both, and we appreciate anything you can do to help us."

The store keeper is very concerned. "What are you and this young man doing on this trail? You don't look like traders."

Bronco takes a deep breath and says, "I apologize. I was so concerned with my young charge that I totally forgot my manners. I'm Bronco Manley. This is one of my young helpers, Jonathan Holley. We are from the settlement of 96. We are tracking a young black man and several Cherokee warriors who stole our guns, ammunition, and supplies. I feel sure they are headed to Keowee. We must be getting close. I'm sure they set the trap that injured Jonathan."

"You and your people have been dealt a hard hand to play. We'll do whatever we can to help you."

The backwoods doctor checks Jonathan. "I'm not a medical doctor, but there's a large knot on the side of the boy's head. He could have a bad concussion. I would like to keep him here for several days if you don't mind. Then, he could continue the journey or return home."

"Thank you, sir. I really do need to be on the move. I appreciate your help with the boy. I'll stop on the way back. Thanks again, sir."

CHAPTER 8

Now that he is traveling alone, Bronco is more determined to catch up with Shad. "I can't drop my guard. Shad could have more traps set for me."

He hears some rustling of leaves above him. As he looks up, he sees a warrior wearing war paint. A terrifying battle cry sends chill bumps up Bronco's spine. He is frozen in his tracks. The young brave leaps and a wrestling match ensues. The outcome is determined by the brute strength of each man. As the match approaches 10 minutes, the advantage switches from the Indian brave to Bronco.

Bronco's arms are like cords of steel. His dad always says that when Bronco gets his 'grizzly bear arms' hooked in a headlock, the other person is down for the count. Once again, another opponent falls.

Bronco barely manages to catch his breath before a second warrior rises from a hole covered with leaves. This Cherokee faces Bronco head on. "I don't have time for this." He looks around for his dad's rifle. He spots it about 25 yards to his left. He dives to his left, and as he rolls, he clasps the rifle. He stands and fires at the warrior who drops in his tracks.

Farther up the trail, Shad realizes his assassins are overdue. This means only one thing. Bronco has defeated his two best warriors. Shad sends the remainder of his group to the village with the stolen goods. He waits for Bronco. It's time for the two gladiators to meet in a final battle; winner takes all. Shad welcomes the meeting.

As Bronco approaches 18 Mile Creek, Shad lies in wait close by. The noise of the river catches Shad's attention. In the distance he sees two small bear cubs playing along the riverbank. They are pushing and shoving, totally absorbed in their favorite game of tag.

A few minutes earlier, Shad scanned the same woods and spotted the cub's den. The mama bear must have been hunting for food close by. Shad knows that it is the wrong time of the year to make contact with a dedicated, protective mama bear. "Perhaps I can use this situation to my advantage. There must be some way I can draw the cubs away from their den. If I can lead them to the path, I can set a trap. Perhaps, the mama bear will take care of Bronco for me."

Shad leaves the shelter of his thicket to search for something that would draw the cubs to the river. He spots a small bee hive in a dead tree. He carefully removes the honeycomb and drips the honey as he moves down the trail. The cubs pick up the scent and begin to follow. In the distance, Shad hears the rumbling of a waterfall.

Unaware of the impending danger, Bronco relaxes on the river bank. He refills his canteen and chews on a piece of deer jerky. He admires the beauty of the area. The river is clear and very deep. He sees rapids in the distance. Judging by the noise, they are rough and very dangerous. With rapids this large, there is usually a waterfall.

He is surprised by a loud rumbling in the bushes.

He hears an angry roar just as a large dark shape emerges. The angry mama bear lunges and misses by only a few feet. He jumps up and runs along the bank of the river.

The vicious creature is clawing and ripping at Bronco's buckskins. He tries to fight her off, but his strength is fading rapidly.

Shad chooses not to watch the murderous display on the part of the bear. He has seen many hunters ripped to pieces. Although he had only met Bronco several times, he admired him. He could hear the angry, rampaging bear and knew that Bronco was no match. Shad has witnessed the slaughtering of a young brave by a very angry bear. This time he chooses to turn and race down the trail in search of his friends. He will let the bear do his dirty work.

Then, out of nowhere, a large chocolate and white dog appears. He is quite a magnificent creature with bulging muscles, sharp claws and large pointed teeth. Without hesitation, without fear, the dog leaps on the bear's back and sinks his teeth deep into the nape of the bear's neck.

Carolina Aussie Rescue

The bear lets out a howl that is heard all over the forest. The bear shakes violently as he tries to break the dog's grip on his neck. The courageous dog simply anchors his claws into the fat that lay beneath the bear's winter coat. The desperate bear begins to roll side to side and over and over, but the dog does not release his death hold.

Bronco tries to stand. But, he's lost a lot of blood. He falls forward just as the bear begins to roll. As the bear flails her mighty paws, one connects with Bronco's head and propels him toward the river. He tries to stand, but he is disoriented and stumbles forward again. He doesn't see the drop to a cliff that overlooks the rapids. He catches his foot on a vine that sends him rolling to the edge. He grabs and he clutches, but he can't find anything to keep him from falling. He slips and tumbles headlong into the treacherous waters.

Bronco refuses to scream. Shad might hear him and return to finish what the bear has started.

Suddenly, the dog releases his hold on the bear and dives into the water. He sinks his teeth into the neck of Bronco's buckskin shirt and wraps his legs around Bronco's torso. Then, the huge dog holds on for the wild ride to come.

The resounding voice of the bear and the battle sounds echo throughout the canyon. Shad looks toward the river just in time to see a strange bundle of fur and buckskin tumbling over the rocks and

rapids. He follows the bundle down the river. He watches as it rolls over the waterfall into the lake below. Then the brave dog drags the lifeless figure toward the riverbank.

A smaller dog could not have pulled the large man up onto the bank. Shad sees the brave, exhausted dog place himself over the limp figure.

Shad approaches the lifeless body. He needs to know that Bronco is dead and is no longer a threat. As Shad nears the body, he hears a low, dangerous growl. The dog sits up and looks Shad in the eye. The dog watches for any threatening movement.

"OK, dog. Good dog. I need to check your friend. He may be badly hurt. I can help him."

The dog doesn't relax his guard position. Shad's only choice is to wait until he's sure that Bronco is dead. Then he can leave the duo alone.

Bronco begins to make some slow movements. The dog

begins to lick his face and nudge him on the shoulder. Bronco groans and turns over slowly. The dog nips at his arms and legs encouraging him to move about. Awake but foggy, he pulls the dog closer and speaks to him as if they are bosom buddies. "You saved me, boy. I was a goner, for sure."

Carefully Shad walks toward the couple. "Hey, man. Your dog won't let me close to you. He's very protective. I saw him pull you out of the river. He's one strong animal. How are you doing?"

"I don't really know. Is this my dog? Did you say he saved me? Why was I in the river?"

"It looks to me like you have a knot on your head. You must have hit your head on some rocks in the river. Do you remember what happened?"

"No, I don't. I do remember a large, angry bear ripping at my clothes. Then, I heard something. It might have been when the dog jumped on the bear. The bear screamed and howled as if it were dying. Then I saw a huge bear paw coming at my head. From that point on, I don't know what happened."

"What's your name, friend?"

Bronco thinks for a few seconds. "I don't know."

This is quite a predicament. Shad stayed with Bronco's family when he was in 96. The townspeople were very nice to him, and they shared stories about Bronco as a young kid and as a man. He is sure Bronco is a good man, and he really doesn't want to hurt him. He studies the dilemma and decides that if Bronco has no memory, he won't need to recover the supplies and return them to 96. Shad can wait a few days to see what develops. He hopes things work out so he doesn't have to kill Bronco right now.

Having made the decision not to kill Bronco, Shad asks, "Do you remember your dog's name? Sometimes people remember their animals and not themselves."

Bronco tries to think. "No, I just don't remember. I have such a headache. I can't stay awake."

Shad knows a concussion is often the result of a blow to the head. "OK, doggy, doggy. This man is hurt and needs my help. You saved him from the bear, the rapids, and the waterfall. If I don't wake him up and keep him awake, he will die. Are you with me or not?"

The dog acts as if he understands what Shad is saying. He backs away far enough for Shad to rouse Bronco and help him to stand. A very low, menacing growl warns Shad to remain on constant guard.

Bronco is far from alert, but he is trying to get his bearings. "What's going on here? Who are you? What is it with this dog? Where am I?"

Not knowing what to say, Shad decides to make it up. "Man, I don't know who you are or where you're going. All I know is this dog loves you, and he's not going to let anything happen to you. But, I can't help you if your dog eats me alive. I'll thank you to tell him that I'm your friend, not your enemy."

"But I don't remember his name."

"He'll probably answer to any name you call him. I didn't see, but I heard him jump on the mama bear that was killing you. So, I reckon we could call him Bear Dog. And since you don't remember your name, maybe we'll call you Bear Man."

"I'm at a complete loss. I don't know where to begin."

Shad looks into the blank eyes and knows he has to help this man. "I live in a Cherokee village not far from here. I'll take you to the medicine man. He helps everyone. Maybe, he can help you."

The two men and the dog travel for about 30 minutes when Shad stops to give Bronco some water. "Man, you are burning up. The bear must have clawed you deep, and the freezing water didn't help. You have a fever."

Shad is helping Bronco walk, but he is becoming exhausted as well. "My village is only a short run from here. At the rate we're traveling, it'll take us two hours to get there. You need some help now. I'm gonna leave you and your dog here. I'll run to my village and bring back a horse."

Bronco speaks with a feverish voice. "You go ahead. I just need to rest a little while. I'll be OK."

"I know you'll be OK. That dog's not gonna let anything get you. I'll be back soon."

Bronco lies on his side. The large chocolate and white dog nestles close to him. The dog's warmth surrounds him like a blanket placed close to a fire until it's toasty warm. The warmth spreads over his body as he falls asleep.

He awakes when he feels the sun shine on his face. There is something heavy on his chest. He opens his eyes to find a large dog stretched over most of his body. "Bear Dog, I don't know where you came from, but you're a good dog! A very good dog!" He pats the dog lovingly as he drifts off to sleep once more.

CHAPTER 9

Bronco opens his eyes. It is very dark and very damp. A wonderful aroma surrounds him and reminds him of the candles his mom makes. She always scents the wax before pouring it into the molds. She mixes special scents for Christmas, Halloween and other notable times. She even makes shapes for special occasions.

"Mom, are you here?" He can barely speak. His lips are dry and swollen. His head is heavy. He feels his heart pounding.

He calls again, "Mom!" There is no answer. This is not his home. He notices a flash of light and hears someone moving around.

"Bear Man," a low feminine voice whispers, "if you'll raise your head, I'll give you some fresh water." He lifts his head a bit. The water is cool and soothing as he swallows a small amount. He doesn't understand what is happening. He looks into a pair of dark eyes that are not his mom's. He's amazed that he remembers his mom's fragrant candles when he can't remember her face or her voice.

He hears the quiet, smooth voice again. "I've been placing cool water on your lips. They are very dry. Try to drink a little more water."

He manages to drink several sips this time. He grabs the hand holding the cup.

"What name did you call me?" The cup falls to the ground. He doesn't realize his own strength.

"Stop, Bear Man. You're hurting my wrist." He releases his grip.

"Where am I?"

"You're inside my family's sweat lodge. You've been very sick. We didn't think you would make it. I've been taking care of you. You're a very strong man with a very strong spirit."

He looks carefully at her face. She has dark skin and sparkling black eyes. Her smile reveals teeth as white as the snow. "How did I come to be here?"

"Shad found you on the riverbank. He and several warriors brought you to our village." She pauses to give him another drink of water. "You were attacked by a bear and knocked into the rapids. Shad said you went over a waterfall."

This is more information than he can process at one time. "Slow down. I remember the bear's large paw coming toward my face. I don't remember anything after that."

The young woman is confused. "You don't remember your dog? He's very much a 'man-god.' You're blessed to have such a strong animal as your spirit guide. He hasn't left your side. He waits outside the door now. It's much too hot in here for him. He hasn't eaten food or drank water since you've been here. If you'll speak to him, he may let me provide him with food and drink."

"You called me Bear Man. What are you calling the dog?"

"Shad said to call him Bear Dog because he fought the bear that attacked you." She becomes very animated in her speech and hand movements. "When the bear knocked you over the cliff, the dog dove into the water to save you. He clung to you as you went over the falls. Then, he pulled you to safety."

"I owe this dog my life. If you'll raise the door cover, I'll speak to him."

The young maiden pulls open the cover and the dog pushes his way in. He crawls on his belly. He starts with Bronco's feet and legs and sniffs the whole man before he lays his head on the broad chest.

Bronco rubs the dog's head and says, "I'm better. Please, let this lady give you food and water. We must regain our strength together."

Bear Dog licks Bronco's face and then crawls back to the opening of the sweat lodge.

Bronco falls back on the pallet. "I owe you for taking care of me. What is your name?"

"My name is Issaqueena. My father is the chief of this village. Bear Dog wouldn't allow Shad to stay near you. Although the Shaman and others approached you, Bear Dog honored me with your care."

"Issaqueena. That is a beautiful name. What does it mean?"

"It means ***deer's head***. The deer is our primary source of food. The ever seeing eye of the deer is our protection. I vigilantly watch for anything that threatens my village."

"Issaqueena, how long have I been here?"

"You've been here for three days. You have several open wounds from the bear. I applied mullein to your wounds to reduce the swelling and infection. You've been breathing mullein smoke from the leaves I put into the fire pit. Your fever has finally broken. You should get better now. I'll get you some food and fresh water. If you like, I'll help you outside so you can eat with your dog." She laughs.

Bronco notices. "You have a beautiful laugh. This must be a happy village."

She nods her head and speaks aloud, "We are very blessed. I hope you'll come to love our village. We'll do all we can to help you regain your health and memory."

Issaqueena helps Bronco through the opening of the sweat lodge. "Oh! The sun is blinding. Is there a shade tree nearby? I must find some shade quickly."

"Calm down, Bear Man. You've had your eyes closed for three days. You can't expect them to adjust immediately."

For the moment Bronco is satisfied. He sits on a nearby stump. Bear Dog walks over and sits beside him. He pets the head of the courageous dog. "It's so strange, Bear Dog. I should remember something as important as you. Just give me time, boy. I'll be fine."

Bear Dog growls. Bronco looks around and sees Shad approaching. "You must be Shad. Issaqueena said the dog wouldn't let you stay near me. Why doesn't Bear Dog like you?"

"I don't know, man. I don't even know the dog. He just picked me out as the one person in the world he hates most. Can you imagine that? No, seriously. How are you feeling today? You've had a rough three days."

"Issaqueena said you found me and brought me to this village. I don't know how I'll be able to thank you. Saying thanks doesn't seem like enough."

"Hey, listen man. You don't owe me anything. I'm just glad you're alive."

"Do you have any idea why I was in the woods? I can't remember who I am or where I belong."

Shad pauses and speaks seriously. "Sometimes it's better not to know who you are or where you're from. My advice is --don't push it. Take your time and enjoy life. You may find this is a new beginning. I did. The Indians here accept people of other races. They don't question or judge. These are truly remarkable people."

"How did you come to be here?"

"I was a slave on a plantation in Charles Town. My dad worked his way up to the important position of black overseer. One night he caught one of the white overseers raping a young slave girl. He beat the white man unconscious. Just unconscious, that's all. He could've beaten and killed a black man and nothing would've been done. My dad knew he would die for his actions. The plantation owner loved my dad, but he couldn't help him. He knew my dad would hang."

Shad has a pained look on his face. "I was my dad's only family. We were important on the plantation. I was eight years old, the same age as Master John's son. I played with Little John. I was in and out of the main house all the time. Heck, I was even included when the teacher came to school Little John. Master John would've been in lots of trouble if someone discovered he was giving me an education."

When Shad pauses, Bronco says, "I didn't know there were slaves who had a good life. I thought all slaves were miserable and mistreated."

"And I thought all slaves had good lives," whispers Shad. "My dad and I had a nice cabin behind the main house. We ate all our meals in the kitchen of the main house. We went to the same church as Master John. I liked my life. I was happy. Then my dad beat the white overseer. Master John didn't wait for the authorities to show up and arrest my dad. He gave us our free papers and made arrangements for us to leave Charles Town. We traveled as far as Keowee where we met the friendly Cherokee who invited us to stay."

"Where is your dad now?"

"He married a maiden from one of the northern tribes. Unlike white folks, Indian husbands move to the woman's tribe. In the Cherokee culture, the woman owns and rules the house. I haven't seen my dad in three or four years. My home is here. I'm a member of this tribe. I'll do anything to help my family. Anything."

"You've had so much pain to carry, but you found peace here. Perhaps I, too, will find peace here. "

CHAPTER 10

Issaqueena approaches with fresh water and soup. "Bear Man, you've been sitting up too long. You're sweaty and pale. Shad, help me get him into the hut."

Once inside the red clay hut, Issaqueena props Bronco on one of the beds so he can be fed some broth. He speaks to her, "You've honored me with your help, but I'd like to feed myself, please."

"Yes, it's time for you to do things for yourself so you'll grow stronger. I'll be outside. Shad, let me know when Bear Man is finished." Issaqueena leaves the hut. She allows Bear Dog to enter and sit next to the bed.

Shad is very nervous around the dog. Bronco questions Shad again, "Why doesn't Bear Dog like you? Did you do something to him?"

"No, man," Shad answers. "I didn't know this dog until I saw him pull you out of the water onto the bank. I helped you walk as far as I could. When I was too weak to help you, I came to the village for some help. The dog allowed Issaqueena and her braves to put you on a stretcher and bring you to this village. He makes me feel very uncomfortable. I'll tell Issaqueena you've finished the broth."

Issaqueena comes into the hut with bear grease, mullein salve, and bandages. "I know this is going to hurt, but I must change the dressings on your wounds. I'll soak them with water first. That should make them easier to remove."

Trying to take his mind off the bandages, Bronco attempts to carry on a conversation. "What is the cream you have with you? It has a very strange odor."

"It's bear grease." Issaqueena begins to laugh. "I'm putting *bear* grease on *Bear* Man as *Bear* Dog looks on."

Bronco joins her laughter. "It appears I have a lot to '*bear*' here."

With her laughter under control, Issaqueena removes the bandages as painlessly as possible. "You have many scratches from the claws of the bear. They aren't healing as well as I hoped. Tomorrow we'll go to the healing springs and scrub the material from the scratches. The hot mineral springs have great healing powers. They cleanse the wounds and prevent infections. I need someone to help you walk to the springs. Shad has volunteered to help. Do you think Bear Dog would allow Shad to help us?"

"I don't know why Bear Dog dislikes Shad, but he'll keep an eye on Shad for us. We'll be safe."

Issaqueena applies the bear grease generously. It burns the flesh where it is applied, and the odor makes Bronco gag. He vomits the water and the broth he has consumed.

"I'm sorry the smell is bad and it has caused you to lose your food. I'll get you some more water and some rabbit to eat. Perhaps that will suit your stomach better."

As she leaves the hut, Bear Dog crawls closer to Bronco which makes him feel very safe and he falls into a deep comfortable sleep.

He awakes several hours later. The sun has set. He sees the fire pit where some meat is roasting. He carefully makes his way out and sits beside the fire.

"I'm pleased to see you getting up on your own," Issaqueena's smile welcomed him to the circle. "This is encouraging. You should be strong enough to travel to the healing waters tomorrow."

Bronco is startled by her beauty and stumbles forward. Isaqueena races to his side to offer her support. He looks deep into large black eyes that reflect the blazes of the fire. Her long black hair shines and her radiant white teeth sparkle. She is an unexpected vision of beauty.

Bronco's heart beats rapidly, and he fears it might explode. He has never been so affected by a woman.

"I'm sorry. I just keep saying that, don't I?"

She looks up into his face and her brilliant smile takes his breath away.

"I don't mind, Bear Man. I'm very strong. I won't let you fall."

Bronco pulls her closer and whispers, "I know you won't let me fall." But he also knows she can't keep him from *falling in love* with her.

CHAPTER 11

"You've rested some, but you need to rest more. We'll make the journey to the healing springs mid-day tomorrow. We'll stay there overnight. Two cleansings should clear the wounds and prevent anymore infection. You may sleep on my cot tonight. I'll sleep here by the fire."

Bronco is again surprised by the strength and beauty of this woman. "No, I don't wish to take your bed from you. I can sleep out here next to the fire." He tries to stand on his own, but he loses his balance and falls back against Issaqueena.

"Bear Man, do as I say and you'll recover. Go against my advice, and you'll grow very weak. Then no one will be able to help you."

Mesmerized by her voice, Bronco agrees to do whatever she says. He turns and walks slowly into the hut. Bear Dog makes himself comfortable in front of the open door. No one else will enter.

Bronco sleeps through the night. It's almost noon when he emerges from the hut. Issaqueena waits for him. She gives him fresh water and bread.

"I've repaired your buckskins. We'll leave as soon as you're ready." She checks her medicine bag once more. She must carry the supplies necessary for his treatment. She has no time for mistakes.

One hour later, Issaqueena calls to Bronco. "Bear Man, it's time for us to go. I've decided to use my horse to carry you and the supplies. Shad and I will take turns leading the horse."

"A horse! This is a welcome surprise. I was worried about walking to the healing springs. I'm relieved. You're a very perceptive young woman."

Shad helps Bronco onto the horse. "Bear Man, I hope you realize what a lucky man you are. Issaqueena has never shown interest in a man. She has always delegated wounded men and suitors to other villagers. The whole village is in an uproar over her actions."

"Believe me, Shad. I realize how lucky I am."

Issaqueena takes the lead line. She speaks to the horse in her native language. She and Shad laugh.

"What did she say, Shad?"

"She told the horse if he didn't throw off the white man, she'd make it up to him."

"Do you think the horse will do what she says?"

"Absolutely! She is in charge of everything in the village. She is #1, top dog, head woman. The chief consults **her** before he consults his council."

Bronco is indeed shocked by this revelation. "I've always known that my mom was really in charge of my family, but I didn't think Indian families worked the same way." He shakes his head; remembering something like that confuses him.

"Women have lots of power in the Cherokee Nation. In this culture the women are considered equal to the men. Not only are they in charge of the family, but they also participate in the government. I've even seen women warriors fight by the side of the fiercest male warriors. And believe me, the women are good at war."

"If the other women are anything like Issaqueena, I wouldn't want to be at war with the Cherokee." He smiles at the thought of fighting against women.

Issaqueena returns from a meeting with her father. She looks angry. "Shad, you lead the horse first. I would like to observe Bear Man's injuries as we travel."

"Yes, m'am." Shad turns and salutes her.

Issaqueena turns her full attention to Bronco. Her bright smile makes him nervous and weak. "Are you able to hold yourself on the horse? If not, I'll ride with you. I don't want you to fall off."

"Let me try on my own. If I feel dizzy, I'll let you know." He prays he can stay on the back of the horse. Her touch might be more than he can resist.

The trio begins the journey. They are covering very little ground.

"We need to reach the springs before nightfall," Issaqueena looks at Bronco as she speaks. "It's important, Bear Man, that you have a treatment today. Your fever is returning. Your wounds must be cleaned."

"I'll do my best to help you get me there." Bronco's eyes are glassy and his speech is slurred.

"Stop, Shad. I'll climb on the horse with Bear Man. He's not able to stay there alone." Shad helps her step up on the horse behind Bronco. She laps her legs over his thighs and sets her feet in front of his knees. She pushes him as far forward as she dares and nestles him against the horse's wide neck.

"I'll keep him balanced. If we fall, we'll make camp and decide what to do."

"Anything you say, m'am," Shad is more worried about Issaqueena than about Bronco.

By the time they reach the healing springs, Issaqueena is almost as weak as Bronco.

"Shad, help me down, please. I can't get down by myself. My legs are numb. I'd help you with Bear Man, but I can't. It'll be a while before I can move normally."

"Don't worry. I can get him down, and then I'll make you both comfortable. You probably would benefit from the healing springs, too. The pool is large enough for two people."

"That's true, Shad. I could cleanse his wounds better if I'm inside the pool. Help me remove his clothes and get him in the pool. I'll gather what I need quickly."

Issaqueena removes her clothing and sits down in

the pool. Shad undresses Bronco and places him with his back to Issaqueena.

Shad unpacks the supplies and cares for the horse.

Issaqueena calls, "Shad, I need your help. I have cleaned the scratches on his back, arms, and chest. I can't reach his legs. I'll hold him while you clean his legs."

Shad completes the task as it grows dark. "I need to gather firewood, but I'll help you get him out of the pool first. Has the healing springs helped you feel better?"

Issaqueena thinks for a moment before saying, "I truly believe they have. I'm no longer exhausted. I've been here many times, but I was neither injured nor exhausted. I simply needed to relax. I'm quite pleased with the springs."

Bronco drifts in and out of consciousness. He rests on a soft pallet. Shad gathers some wood and starts a fire. Issaqueena has packed soup stock and bread. She will have a meal ready soon.

Bronco opens his eyes and looks around. He sees a woman stirring something in a small pot over a bright fire. A large man sits opposite him. The smell of hickory burning and the aroma from the pot intrigues him.

As he shifts his weight, Bronco feels a warm presence against him. Bear Dog lifts his head and places it on Bronco's chest. "Well, boy, this is a pleasant surprise."

As he rubs the dog's back, he speaks toward the fire. "Are we at the healing springs?"

Isaqueena turns toward him, "The soup will be ready in just a few minutes. I have some bread and herbal tea to make you more alert."

As she rises, he briefly recalls the feel of the warm waters as he leans back into the arms of a beautiful woman. Her hands roam over his arms and chest. She softly nudges him forward and caresses the muscles on his back. She, no, someone lifts his leg, but the touch is not the same. He wants to pull his leg away, but he doesn't have the strength.

A soft hand is placed on his forehead and then softly caresses his face. His chin is lifted and she looks deeply into his eyes. "You're much cooler, and your eyes are clear. The healing springs are helping.

I'll check your scratches in the morning. One more time in the springs might be enough. If you're not better, we will stay one more night so you can have two more treatments."

"Thank you. I'm feeling much better. I'm remembering someone in the pool with me. Was that person you?"

"Yes. You were too weak to sit up by yourself. Rather than let you drown, I cleaned your wounds from within the pool. I'm not sure what tomorrow will bring. But for now, you must eat and drink to grow stronger."

Shad comes toward Bronco. When he hears Bear Dog growl, he searches for the dog's location then sits on a stump a few feet away.

"You do look better, man. You've come closer to death than anyone I ever saw. You must have an angel on your shoulder."

"Perhaps, but I think I have an angel here on earth. Issaqueena has a glow that I haven't seen on anyone before. What made her pick me to save?"

"I don't know. I've heard stories about her psychic powers. She knows things before they happen. Some people in the village said she knew you were coming. They didn't want her to help you. The Cherokee has many problems with the white man. They have been lied to, cheated out of their land, and even murdered. I don't blame them for disliking all white men. Who can tell which white man is good or which is bad?"

"I remember hearing about the broken treaties and the mistreatment of the Cherokee, but I can't see the face of the person who told me. This amnesia is difficult to understand. I don't know what to expect."

"Well, Bear Man, I hear that some people get their memory back as soon as their head wounds heal. I also hear that some people never get their memory back. Sometimes an incident, a person, or a location jars the memory, and it all comes back. It's a waiting game."

"I have no other choice. I'll wait, but I don't think I'm good at waiting."

After a nourishing meal, Bronco is ready for some much needed rest. Issaqueena makes sure his pallet is as comfortable as possible.

Shad takes care of the fire. He stokes it several times during the night under Bear Dog's watchful eye.

CHAPTER 12

The next morning is warm and clear.

Bronco watches as Issaqueena prepares a simple breakfast of herbal tea and hoecakes. He's hungrier than he expected. He could eat several hoecakes, but he is afraid his stomach might not like so much food at once.

"This hoecake is really good, ma'm."

She seems offended, "Call me Issaqueena, please. I don't like being ma'med."

Bronco is surprised and changes the subject. "You thought of everything we would need on this trip. Do you think one more time in the waters will be enough?"

"Let me check your wounds. Your arms and back are much better. The scratches on your stomach do not look as good. Take off your pants so I can check your leg wounds."

"Excuse me? What?" Bronco stammers.

"Bear Man, you didn't wear clothes in the pool last night, and you won't wear them today. What's the matter? Are you shy? Shad and I removed your pants last night, so nothing will surprise us." Issaqueena begins to giggle.

Then Shad laughs out loud. "Will we have to knock you out to get your clothes off? You didn't seem to mind last night while Issaqueena doctored on you."

Bronco pales. "Was she in the pool? Was she naked, too?"

There's much giggling and loud laughter at Bronco's expense. Issaqueena giggles so much she has hiccups and can't speak. Shad falls on the ground holding his belly and kicking his feet into the air. Several minutes pass before Shad has enough control to say, "You bet she was, and you were too passed out to notice."

Issaqueena giggles even harder. She has to sit down on a stump or fall down on the ground like Shad. She manages to squeak, "Bronco does not like naked." She collapses again.

Bronco turns his back to the laughing duo and removes his pants. "How do the scratches on my leg look? Feel free to examine them as I walk away." He points at Issaqueena, "I'll be waiting in the pool when your laughing spasm is over."

She giggles so much she cries. She asks, "May I take my clothes off, too?"

"That's up to you. I can scrub all the scratches except the ones on my back. I'll need help with them."

He pauses as he turns to the dog. "Bear Dog, perhaps you can scrub my back. These two will laugh until they make themselves sick. What do you say, boy?"

Bear Dog wags his tail, but he doesn't bark.

Shad coughs, "His rough tongue could substitute for the coral sponge Issaqueena used last night. It might even be better."

Bronco casually walks to the healing springs and climbs in. "Wow! This water is hot! Did you say it has minerals that help the healing?"

A few minutes later, Issaqueena walks over to the pool. She tries to maintain an air of self-confidence. "I would like to clean the wounds on your back."

With a straight face, Bronco asks, "Do you think you can clean them without laughing?"

He waits until he's sure she has her laughter under control. "I'm beginning to feel both used and abused."

He pretends to cry. "Nobody loves me!"

He extends his hand seeking comfort. He looks deeply into Issaqueena's eyes. She gives him her hand, and he jerks her into the pool.

She gags and spits out the mineral water left in her mouth.

A slow, brilliant smile spreads over Bronco's face. "Now it's my turn to laugh." And laugh he does.

At first Issaqueena's face is blank. Then the realization of what Bronco has done starts her giggling again. Shad can only look on.

He is laughing so hard that he can barely stand. He doesn't dare try to walk.

Bronco says, "Oh, my gosh. She's giggling again. If she falls down in this pool, she might drown. Help! Help!"

Bear Dog comes running. He leaps into the pool and begins to swim around.

Bronco attempts to speak through his laughter. "Look! Even Bear Dog's smiling and wagging his tail. He's laughing in dog language."

Shad runs toward the pool. Bear Dog stops swimming and growls. Shad stops dead in his tracks.

"That dog spoils all my fun! What does he have against me? What did I ever do to that dog?" Shad finds a nearby stump and sits down. He pouts while Bear Man, Bear Dog and Issaqueena splash water and play.

Bronco surrenders. "Whoa! I give up! Woman! Dog! Stop! I've been very sick. I'm still very weak. I'm afraid I might slip under the water and drown."

Issaqueena asks, "You *were* unconscious last night, weren't you? Or did you pretend to be unconscious so I'd stay in the pool with you? You don't play fair."

"I promise I didn't trick you. This morning I remembered a little of the pool incident, but I didn't remember you being naked."

"You're so funny, but I do need to clean your wounds. Turn around, please."

"OK. But don't keep telling me to turn around. I get dizzy easily. I've been sick, you know."

"Stop your silly talk, Bear Man. We need to be serious about your wounds. I'm glad to see these scratches are clean of the infection that caused the fever. We'll go back to the village after we finish here."

She looks around for Shad. He is already packing up. "Shad is breaking down the camp. We'll be able to leave in an hour or so. I've cleaned your back. Now I'll climb out and help Shad. Get ready, please."

"I'd like to walk back to the village with you, Shad, and Bear Dog."

Delicately Issaqueena speaks, "I don't think that's a good idea. You're still very weak. If you walk, you'll become exhausted again and could have a major set-back."

"All right, I'll ride the horse back to the village, but I'd like to hold the reins in my hands. I feel better if I'm not led."

"I understand. I agree to you having the reins."

CHAPTER 13

Issaqueena is leading the group back to the village. Shad walks beside the horse Bronco has been guiding. The reins fall from the horse.

Slowly Bronco speaks, "Shad, I'm not feeling very well." Then he follows the reins to the ground. Shad cushions the fall as best he can.

Issaqueena turns, "Bear Man, what is wrong?"

She tenderly touches his forehead. He is hot and sweaty. "Shad, let's drag him over to the side of this path. I will get the blankets and the spring's water so we can cool him down."

"Bear Man," she speaks gently, "your fever has returned. We must break this fever. If we can't do this, we'll go back to the spring. Can you hear me?"

Bronco mumbles incoherently.

"Don't worry," she says. "It's not unusual for a low fever to return shortly after the wounds are cleaned. We can take care of it right here on the path."

She and Shad wrap Bronco in blankets. Issaqueena wets a soft cloth with the healing spring's water. She wipes Bronco's forehead and neck.

About an hour later, Bronco stops shivering and falls into a restful sleep. Bear dog has watched silently. Now he crawls over to Bronco and nestles into his side.

"I think he'll be OK, Shad. We'll camp here tonight."

Shad speaks, "I'll gather some wood for a fire. You sit here and rest. You look very tired. This has been very hard on you. Do we need to go back to the healing waters?"

"Let's wait until he wakes, then we'll make the decision."

When Shad returns with the wood, Issaqueena, Bronco and Bear Dog are sleeping peacefully. Shad builds a fire and starts some herbal tea and corn soup. He waits for over an hour.

He mumbles to himself, "No one else is awake, so I'm going to eat my supper. I'll fix theirs if they wake up later."

Bronco and Issaqueena sleep through the night. The next morning brings a beautiful day.

Shad hurries the preparation of breakfast. "All right, people. It's time to be on the road. We're wasting daylight. Eat! Chomp! Chomp!"

Bronco moans a little as he removes the blankets and stands slowly. "I feel much better. I can make the trip now."

Issaqueena touches his forehead. "I agree. We'll try again."

She and Shad break camp and load the horse.

She looks at Shad, "I'll walk beside the horse, Shad. You lead."

The group stops to rest several times. The sun is setting as they enter the village. Everyone turns. Some wave, some nod their heads, but no one speaks.

"Shad, please show Bear Man where he is to stay." Issaqueena walks toward the Council House.

"Come with me, Bear Man. I'll show you where you'll be living."

Bronco is confused. "What exactly will be my role in this village?"

Shad laughs. "Everyone not born into a clan must start at the bottom. You'll play the role of a farmer and work with the women as they plant the seeds and harvest the crops. In the fall you'll gather nuts and prepare food for storage. Pounding corn into flour is a difficult job, but you have the muscles for it. You'll like tanning the hides of animals, but I'm not sure how you'll fare when trying to make those same hides into clothing."

Bronco stops. "I recognize this building. It's the sweat lodge where I first awoke. And this is Issaqueena's hut. I assume I won't be staying here."

"Logical assumption, Bear Man." Shad led Bronco to the rear of the hut. "I'll show you the lean-to. This is where you'll bed down at night. You'll hang your bedroll on this hook while you work all day."

Shad pauses. "Idle hands aren't allowed. There's no time for sitting. In the case of torrential rain, you may be allowed to sleep in the sweat lodge. And if it's extremely cold, you may be allowed to sleep in the sweat lodge. But, take my advice, don't ask to sleep there. Issaqueena will tell you when it's allowed. I'll find you a bedroll before nightfall. For now, you're to report to the fields. I'll walk you there."

"Thanks, Shad. It's difficult not knowing who I am or where I belong. Believe me, I'm not afraid of hard work. In fact, I welcome the chance to stay busy."

CHAPTER 14

As they walk into the fields, Bronco asks, "Why are there so many people in the village? There weren't so many when we left for the springs."

"There are seven clans in this Cherokee village. The visitors are members of the other six clans. Villages have local festivals so young people can meet since it's forbidden to marry someone of your own clan."

"What exactly is our clan?"

"This is the Paint clan. Its members use red paint to decorate their bodies. They're taught the healing ways from childhood. Many of them study sorcery and become the medicine men and women. Other tribes come here for medical and mental care. This is the reason I brought you to Issaqueena. She's the chief medicine woman of this village. She knows what to do when someone is hurt as badly as you."

Shad proudly states, "I was adopted into the Blue clan. We make medicine from the blue colored plant. I've been moved to the Paint clan, temporarily, to take care of you. When your place is finalized, I'll return to my people in the Blue clan."

Several minutes of silence pass. "We're almost at the fields. I'll introduce you to the woman in charge. I'll hang around to interpret for you and explain how you're to do the work. But, I'd like to make one thing clear. This is like a vacation for me. I intend to sit in the shade, drink water, and flirt with all the beautiful maidens. Perhaps, I'll find my future wife in this clan."

"Are you seriously looking for a wife?"

"Well, yes, I am. I don't like sleeping alone in the winter or anytime. I like having someone to talk to and make plans for the future. I'd like to have a complete family, kids and everything. I don't think that's asking too much. How about you, Bear Man?"

"I'm not even thinking in that direction. My plan is to find out who I am and where I belong. Then I'll go from there."

The woman in charge walks out to meet them. Shad takes the maid aside and speaks to her quietly for several minutes before turning to Bronco. "Bear Man, this is Loving Woman. You'll be working with her." He turns to Loving Woman. "Where would you like him to start?"

"Need pulling corn, but he big man. Be hard him go up rows. Use him carry baskets to wagon. He leave empty basket end of row. Women fill again. He come back, leave empty basket, take full one."

Loving Woman returns to her task. Shad explains, "The corn rows are very long. Each worker is assigned to pull the corn between two rows. She pulls the ears from her right and her left, and she places them in a shoulder pouch. When the pouch is full, she walks back to the end of the row and empties the pouch into the basket. She reenters her row to fill her pouch again. When her basket is full, she carries it to the wagon to empty. She returns to her rows and starts again. Loving Woman would like to try a different method because you are too large to go between the corn rows. What she would like for you to do is replace the full basket with an empty one, carry the full basket to the wagon, empty it, and return to the rows to exchange the empty basket for a full basket. Whew! Do you get my drift?"

"I understand what Loving Woman wants me to do. While the two of you talked, I have been observing the actions of the women. There is too much wasted movement. I can come up with a better method for Loving Woman's crew. I'll do basically what she has suggested. But after the women stop, I'll need your help to do some remodeling of this corn patch."

The strength and the capacity of the baskets surprise Bronco. Their sturdiness enables him to run a rope through the handles of one basket, across his shoulders, and through the handles of a second basket. He empties the baskets and then exchanges them for two more full baskets. Once again he runs the rope through the handles of one full basket, then over his shoulders and through the handles of a second full basket. He is carrying twice the amount of corn and freeing the women from stopping their work to carry their baskets to the wagon.

Loving Woman stops Bronco, "You very strong. Very good worker. Save time. Pick much more corn."

Other than Issaqueena, she is the first Indian to speak to him.

He scans the tree line in search of Shad. The action feels familiar somehow. He motions for Shad.

"If you don't mind helping out, we can get these women caught up so we can work on my idea before sunset."

"No, man! I told you this is like a vacation for me. I'm not required to work."

"Shad, if you help me, you'll be working very close to the single women. They'll be very thankful for your help. This could be your chance to meet the love of your life."

"Umm…" Shad thinks about it. "I guess I could help out. Do you really think the women will like me?"

"How could they not? You're tall and strong, maybe even handsome. Your skin is dark. Do you sing? A beautiful voice always impresses the ladies."

"That's true. The slaves sang as they worked. The males with the best voices could have any woman they wanted. I can be romantic and sing for the women. Hey, I need a piece of rope so I can carry two baskets like you. I want them to see my muscles flexing as I do more work than you."

"There you go, Shad. I knew you would come around."

Loving Woman is surprised and amazed to see how much faster the women's work is completed. The women are able to pull all the ready ears of corn on the rows. The wagon is full. Bronco's idea proved that filling the pouch is not the laborious part of pulling corn. Carrying the large basket from the end of the row to the wagon is the strenuous part. Today the women aren't as tired as they walk back to the village. When the wagon stops at the workstation where the corn will be shucked, everyone is excited and ready for the cleaning.

Loving Woman proudly approaches Shad and Bronco. "You make our work easy today. Lots of corn."

Bronco smiles. He is proud to have eased their work. He bows his head to her and speaks, "I'm glad I could help."

CHAPTER 15

Bronco and Shad walk to their lean-to behind Issaqueena's hut. They prepare their own little meal. It is understood that Bronco and Shad can't eat with the family until invited to do so.

After eating, Bronco and Shad return to the corn field. "If we remove the rocks and debris along both sides of the corn field, we can build a system of ropes and pulleys that will connect the baskets."

"Why do we need to clean the tracks by picking up the rocks and debris? That's hard work, and I'm on vacation."

"Oh, stop your whining, Shad. We will be suspending the baskets close to the ground, and I don't want any rocks or debris interfering with the basics' movement. We will space the baskets according to the space of the rows. The rope system will pull the baskets to the wagon parked at the front of the field, not the side. We empty the baskets and return them to the other side of the pulley. It will be a continuous circle of baskets. This should shorten the time needed for pulling and processing the corn."

"It all sounds good when you say it. But, Bear Man, this is supposed to be my vacation. You keep using that 'we' word. I didn't sign up to be a part of your 'we'." Shad complains all the way to the corn field where he immediately starts clearing rocks and debris.

"There's a full moon. We could work through the night and surprise the ladies with our invention tomorrow."

"Bear Man, do you ever get tired? Since the fever broke and we returned to the village, you've been wide open. I need some rest."

Bronco laughs. "I've heard that many times. My philosophy is: If the sun is up, time to work. If the sun is down, time to sleep. If there is a full moon, do whatever work requires very little light."

"Well, I tell you right now. I don't like that philosophy. My philosophy is: Do the least amount of work required to stay alive."

"I don't believe you. Once you get started, you seem to work well."

"Man, I really have you fooled, don't I? Don't answer that."

Bronco assures him, "When you see the maidens' faces light up tomorrow, it will be worthwhile."

The duo removes the rocks and debris and sets up a series of stakes and ropes to complete the pulley system needed to move the baskets on an oblong path.

Loving Woman arrives first. Her eyes reflect disbelief and confusion. Bronco demonstrates the pulley system and attempts to explain how it can increase production. She can't follow what he is saying.

Shad takes Loving Woman aside and speaks to her in Cherokee. When they return, she understands enough to tell her maidens how it works.

"Shad, I have noticed that no one speaks to me. You, Issaqueena, and Loving Woman speak English. It makes sense that you should speak to me, but no one speaks Cherokee when I'm around. Several times you've whispered to or taken aside those who speak only Cherokee. Just a few minutes ago, you took Loving Woman aside to explain all this in Cherokee. I'd like to learn to speak the language."

"I'm sorry, Bear Man. You were badly hurt. The only way Issaqueena would agree to help was if I stayed with you at all times, and no one spoke to you in Cherokee. She's protecting her territory and her people."

"I understand she's protecting her territory, but, there's more to it than that."

"OK. Time out. The beautiful maidens approach." Shad preens like a peacock. "I find them much more appealing than discussing who speaks English and who speaks Cherokee."

Loving Woman and Shad divide the ladies into two groups and assign their rows. They understand the process enough to put it to work immediately. Everyone is excited and works hard to do exactly as told.

Loving Woman finds Bronco. She pats him on the back, "Good man. Thank you."

This is a special moment for Bronco. He has made a good friend in Loving Woman.

CHAPTER 16

The next morning Bronco and Shad ready the pulleys once more. The ready corn is gathered several hours earlier than expected. As the corn wagon and the workers come in from the field, the villagers gather to cheer and honor the accomplishment. Many nod to Bronco. Some shake his hand. Several wave.

"Do you think they'll accept me for my merits now?"

"No, they won't. Individuals might like you, but they'll do exactly what the white chief tells them."

"What is a white chief?"

"Bear Man, you ask too many questions, and you make me feel like a history teacher. Now, listen closely. Each tribe has two chiefs, the white chief and the red chief. The white chief leads the people in times of peace. This peace chief has an able council to help rule. The red chief leads in times of war. If there is no war, the red chief has nothing to do except train himself and his warriors to respond instantly to threats pertaining to war."

"Good answer, Shad. Who is the white chief?"

A smile crosses Shad's face and a laugh escapes from his throat. "Issaqueena is the white chief, and she decided that you would be saved. She makes all the decisions and issues all the orders pertaining to you. If the tribe had been at war when we arrived, the red chief would have made the decision."

"Come on, Shad. Do I have to pull every bit of information out of you a little at a time? Who is the red chief?"

"Issaqueena's father, War Eagle. He is very angry at the way the white man has been treating the tribes. He would've put you to death."

"What happens if a war breaks out while I'm still here in the village?"

"If you've shown the tribe that you are sincere and non-threatening, then you'll be left with Issaqueena. If War Eagle judges you a threat, then he'll execute you. The fact that you have no memory of your past life is important because you have nothing to stop you from becoming a member of the tribe. But understand this, you'll never be allowed to leave this tribe alive. You join, you stay, or you die. End of story."

"Gosh, Shad. You paint a grim picture of my future, but thank you for being honest with me."

"Both War Eagle and Issaqueena are impressed with what you've done with the corn crop. It shouldn't be difficult for you to gain acceptance if that is what you desire. The chiefs will set a time limit to your visitation here before you are required to make a choice. Just remember my warning."

"I will. Meanwhile, will you teach me the Cherokee language?"

"No. I follow Issaqueena's orders. She must give me permission to teach you the language. I brought you here to save your life, but I'll not go against Issaqueena."

"So be it. Tell me, Shad. How do I get to see Issaqueena? I haven't seen her since we returned from the healing springs."

"Again, Bear Man. I can't help you there. She'll seek you out when she is ready. Good luck."

CHAPTER 17

Bronco and Shad help complete the corn harvest in record time. The ladies have more time to prepare for the visitors. The Cherokee take great pride in entertaining. Hospitality is carefully planned with lots of food and drink available. Comfort is at the top of the list. Issaqueena's Paint clan is the host for this year's Green Corn Ceremony. She is busy overseeing the preparations.

Bronco looks for Shad. He has a few questions to ask.

"Shad, put yourself in history teacher mode again. I wish to ask some questions."

"OK," Shad grins as he turns. "I'm getting good at this professor thing."

"Why are there even more men and women in the village today?"

"Every year all seven clans take part in the Green Corn Ceremony. We celebrate the completion of the harvest of the first ripened corn. This year has been a bumper crop for this clan. Word of your pulley system has spread. The other clans are anxious to see how it works. Loving Woman will be the center of attention as she demonstrates it. She's very proud and will do you great honor as the inventor."

Shad points to the young ladies giggling as they walk to the village. "The young girls are excited because many young bucks are here for the four day ceremony. The maidens view these ceremonies as a chance to flirt and possibly make choices for life partners. There will be dancing in the Ceremonial Grounds, and many games will be played between the clans. Rivalry carries over from year to year. The white man calls it 'bragging rights'. "

"Can anyone compete in the games? Will you be competing with your Blue Clan?"

"As a matter of fact, yes." Shad pats himself on the back. "I helped my clan to be the overall champion last year. Stickball is my game. If you wish to compete, you must have Issaqueena's permission. She could sponsor you as a prospective member of her clan. If the other clans agree, you'll be allowed to compete."

"Will you help me locate Issaqueena so I can ask about the games?"

"Sure, I'll help you. Nothing would suit me better than playing against you. That would be a competition all the clans would enjoy."

They search the village for Issaqueena. Everyone they meet smiles and waves to them. Loving Woman is speaking to some of the young maidens.

As they approach, Shad calls out, "Loving Woman, we are looking for Issaqueena. Have you seen her nearby?"

Loving Woman carefully answers, "She near Council House."

Shad bows his head to Loving Woman as a sign of honor. "Thank you, Loving Woman."

They walk toward the Council House where they meet Issaqueena. Shad motions Bronco to be silent. "Issaqueena, it has been many days since speaking with you. I wish to ask for your approval on a matter."

"It's nice to see you again, Shad." She turns to Bronco and smiles. "It's nice to see you, too, Bear Man. I have heard good things about your work in the corn field. I thank you for your help."

She returns her attention to Shad. "What is your question?"

"The Green Corn Ceremony is beginning. The games are very competitive. As you know, I belong to the Blue Clan, and I'll play for them. Bear Man has no clan, but he would like to compete. Which clan could he represent?"

"Very interesting question." She turns to Bronco. "Bear Man, would you like to play in the games?"

"I'd welcome the chance to compete."

"Is there a clan you would like to represent?"

Bronco smiles, "I would like to represent the Paint clan. The members have become my family here in the village. They know me. I'd be proud to represent them in the games."

She bows her head in recognition of his request. "I will speak to the other white chiefs. If they approve, you'll be allowed to play."

She turns to Shad, "Is there anything else?"

"No, Issaqueena, thank you for your help."

He turns to Bronco, "Well, good buddy. She'll probably help you get into the games. I'll be waiting on the field with my clan. I'll be happy to explain the rules if you get to play."

Bronco grins and offers his hand. "Let's shake on it, Shad. This should make for some interesting games."

"I agree. But, right now let's stroll through the visitors' area. I would like to scope out some good looking ladies. You might keep your eyes open as well. Many of the ladies are scoping both of us, you know."

"I'm sure you're correct, but not many of them speak English. That makes it difficult for me to talk to them."

Shad laughs, "When you're right, you're right. There's nothing like a language barrier to keep you from getting to know one of these beautiful ladies. Sorry, Bear Man."

"Not as sorry as I am," Bronco agrees. "I'll just find me a spot to stand and watch as you charm the ladies."

"Perhaps you can learn something. Just watch this 'ladies man' show you how it's done."

CHAPTER 18

A short time later, the seven clans enter the Ceremonial Grounds. Each clan has a section marked by its ceremonial mask. Everyone wears the best robes and hats owned. A new sacred fire is lit in the center. At one point in the four day celebration, all fires in the village will be put out and relit from this sacred fire.

It is very warm and humid as Bronco watches the fashion parade. Buckskin shirts and pants are decorated with colorful beads. The white and red chiefs of each clan wear elaborate robes made from deer, elk, and buffalo. Their robes are decorated with the feathers from the eagle and other birds. Their headpieces are fox, coyote, and bear.

Bronco hears the chiefs as they tell of their accomplishments since the last gathering of the clans. Bronco doesn't understand what they are saying because all of them speak in their Cherokee language. When Issaqueena makes her speech, she mentions Bear Man's name several times. He can't tell if she is talking about his method for harvesting the corn or if she is asking permission for him to compete in the games.

Ceremonial Grounds
Cherokee, NC

It takes many hours for all the white chiefs and red chiefs to speak. All clans sit respectfully. No one speaks while the chiefs are speaking. No one stands up or leaves the Ceremonial Grounds. Bronco is amazed at the fortitude of the adults and the children.

After the last speaker, the chiefs leave their clans and once again parade through the village. For the moment, they are free to walk, to relax, to eat. Issaqueena stands apart from the council. She spots Bronco outside the Ceremonial Grounds. She smiles as she walks to him.

"There were no objections to you playing for my clan. Several of the chiefs thought you would add to the rivalries that already exist. Cherokee men love to wager. You're the unknown factor which makes everything more interesting. Believe me when I say, the games are a very important part of our existence. Do not take your eyes off your opponents. Do not show mercy. These games are practice for real battles. The warriors hone their skills and fight as if to the death. Take nothing for granted."

"Thank you, Issaqueena. I appreciate your help. I won't let you down."

Bronco walks to his lean-to, gathers his bedroll, and attempts to rest for the remainder of the night. He will need his strength for the games.

The clans gather early. All ballplayers attend the ceremony. One woman from each clan dances around the center of the Ceremonial Grounds. During the dance, the women stomp on black beads that represent players of the opposing team.

The partying has begun. There is dancing, singing, feasting, and praying for divine support. This continues through the night. Tomorrow the games begin. They will last from sunup to sundown.

Bronco walks toward Shad who is on the opposite side of the fire. "When can you help me with the rules of the games?"

"Usually opponents don't fraternize before a big game, but I'll make an exception for you. Stickball is the tribe's favorite game and is referred to as 'little brother to war'. The warriors are tough and competitive. Arms and legs may be broken tomorrow. There have even been some deaths. Often a game of stickball has settled disputes between tribes."

Shad leads Bronco to the Ceremonial Grounds where game

supplies are stored. Shad speaks to the guard who allows them to study some of the supplies. "Each warrior is given two hickory sticks with a pouch on the end." Shad demonstrates how the sticks are to be held. "Female players use their hands instead of sticks. Each clan has a medicine man. One of the medicine men tosses a small ball like this one into the air. The ball is made of deer hide and hair. You catch the ball in one of these pouches. Then, you throw it toward the goal as hard as you can."

They walk to the field that has been readied for play. "The goal is this wooden pole. Do you see the fish carved on the top?"

He waits for Bronco to see the top. "This pole is approximately twenty-eight feet tall. Do you see the score line near the top?"

Shad pauses again. "If the ball hits above the score line, the team scores seven points. If the ball hits below the score line, the team scores two points. When points are scored, the teams reassemble. The medicine men alternate tossing the ball to restart the game."

Bronco absorbs the information then asks, "How many points in a game?"

Shad explains, "Before the game, the council decides on the number of points needed to complete the game. The first team to reach set number wins."

"You mentioned injuries. How are they handled?"

"Other than the ball toss after each score, the game does not stop until set number is achieved. If someone is injured, he continues to play until he can no longer move. If he falls to the ground, his clan's medicine man will send waiting warriors onto the field to remove the injured player. There is no shame in being carried from the game. There is only shame if the warrior gives up and removes himself from the game. The injured player's matched warrior on the team must leave the game, also. Remaining players continue until the points are earned or no warriors are left. You may live to regret playing in the games, Bear Man."

"I don't fear physical contact. I just want to know how much I can hurt someone and not be penalized." They both laugh, but there is an underlying truth to the statement.

CHAPTER 19

The party lasts throughout the night. Everyone except Bronco eats too much, dances too much, sings too much, and does not sleep. Despite the noise and the movement, Bronco finds a comfortable place where he can nap through the night.

Shad crawls to the area where Bronco sleeps. A low growl warns Bronco that someone is approaching. "Wake up, Bear Man. Call off your dog. The games start in one hour. All seven clans play. The medicine men will draw stones to determine who plays whom. Players are expected to be there for the tossing. What are you going to do with your dog during the games?"

"I'm going to place him in Issaqueena's hut and pull the rails across the doorway. I'll tell him to stay. He'll stay. Bear Dog does as I say." He rubs Bear Dog's head. He still can't remember how the dog fits into his past, but he is sure the dog is a part of his future.

Bronco and Bear Dog walk past the warriors. Some are passed out. Many begin to awake. Bronco watches the medicine men ready the participants for the stickball game. First, a black tea made from mushrooms is served warm.

Each warrior drinks the tea, vomits, and then begins to stretch his arms and legs. After this cleansing, the medicine men bless the warriors. The warriors separate into clans for final preparations for the games. They will meditate until their medicine men return with the schedule for the stickball games.

At the Council House the medicine men are given a number. They draw stones that have marks to represent numbers 1-7. The first medicine man to draw his own number will secure a 'by' for his clan. This means his team will not play in the first round. Their first game will be played in the second round.

Bronco's clan, the Paint clan, wins the 'by' and the schedule is determined.

The Long Hair clan is known as the 'Peace Chiefs'. In times of peace, this clan has the most control of the tribe.

Issaqueena is of the Paint clan who are sorcerers and medicine people who decorate their bodies with red paint. Male members marry into clans where they are needed.

The Bird clan is the 'keeper of the birds'. They use blowguns and snares to capture or kill the birds needed within the tribe.

The Wolf clan is the 'War Chiefs' who specialize in fighting. They develop strategies and stay in good physical shape should a war begin.

The Wild Potato clan is the foragers and gatherers of potatoes. They are thought of as the food suppliers and share with other clans when needed.

The Deer clan boasts the fastest runners and the best deer hunters.

Shad is a member of the Blue clan who makes medicine from the blue colored plants.

The Medicine Men determine the schedule for the games.

Game one: The Long Hair clan against the Wolf clan.

Game two: The Bird clan against the Wild Potato clan.

Game three: The Deer clan against the Blue clan.

Bronco is glad his clan has the 'by'. He will watch three games before his clan plays. By then he must be ready to play.

Bronco leads Bear Dog to Issaqueena's hut and places him inside. "Bear Dog, I'm participating in the stickball competition. You can't be there. You'd be upset and run onto the field. You must not do that. You stay inside and wait for my return."

Bear Dog slowly walks to the back corner of the room and curls up. He covers his head with his front paws. He will do as Bronco says.

Bronco meets Issaqueena as he walks back to the field. "Thank you for allowing me to place Bear Dog in your hut. He won't mess up anything. He's a very good dog."

She smiles brightly, "Yes, he is a very good dog. I've never met a dog like him. He is truly devoted to you. It would be difficult for him to watch you play."

Bronco smiles at her, "Our clan is very fortunate to draw the 'by' for the first round. Would it be possible for you to sit with me during the games? Shad's playing for his clan, and I need someone to explain the game."

"Are you using your wily charms on me?"

He stammers a bit, "No, I wouldn't use my charms on you." He takes a deep breath, "That wasn't what I meant to say. I'd charm you if given the chance, but... That didn't sound right either."

Issaqueena laughs, "So, I must wait until you know who you are before you will work your charms on me. Is that what you said?" She blushes and her whole face appears to brighten. "Would you like to start this conversation over?"

"Yes, I would." Bronco tries to stand still but can't. "I'm just digging myself deeper and deeper every time I speak."

He bows properly, "I would appreciate your company during the games today. I'm sure you'll teach me the rules of the game so I can represent our clan well."

"Since you put it so nicely, I'll be honored to join you at the stickball field."

Bronco extends their conversation by asking, "Is this particular field used every year?"

"No. The council chooses a large field close to the host clan's village. We're the host clan, so they've chosen a field to our south.

There's a beautiful mountain stream on the south side of the field. A work crew has set the goal posts at each end of the field. They are expertly crafted with a wooden fish on the top. The poles are 28 feet high. If the stickball hits the top of the post, the team earns seven points. If the player hits below the top mark, the team earns only two points. The clan medicine man sticks the number of counting pegs in the ground for all to see. The first clan to reach 12 counting pegs wins."

She pauses, "Do you have another question, Bronco?"

"Yes. How many players are on the field at one time?"

She explains expertly, "Each clan sends 10 warriors onto the field. The warriors of one clan are paired up with warriors of similar height, weight, and build from the opposing side. When a warrior leaves the field, his paired mate must leave the game, also."

Issaqueena apologizes, "This is much to understand. The game starts with 20 men. The chosen captain goes to the center where a medicine man tosses the ball into the air. Mayhem breaks out all over. There are no rules of conduct; anything goes -biting, choking, gouging, scratching, twisting of arms and legs, and banging each other over the head with the wooden racket. There are no timeouts, no substitutes. Once the game begins, it doesn't stop until one team has 12 pegs. If two teams are well matched, a game could last from dawn to dusk."

"Is there wagering on the games?"

"Oh, yes. Too much. It's not uncommon for a man to lose his horse and even the shirt on his back. Gambling is a detrimental affliction of my race."

Bronco asks again, "Will you watch the games with me?"

She hesitates a little, "I don't usually come to the games. I spend most of my time with the weavers. I like to study the different techniques. If I can find an opening in my schedule, I'll come to the games and sit with you."

"OK." Bronco is disappointed, but he manages to smile.

CHAPTER 20

The first game is totally one sided. The Long Hair clan has become soft over the years. They don't score any points against the Wolf clan. The game lasts less than one hour. The Long Hair clan is so ashamed of its performance that it packs up and returns home. The remaining games will be played without them.

The second game is a little more competitive. The Bird clan members work well together. They are more physically fit than the Wild Potato clan. Bronco is happy to see more action. He watches as the players use their rackets to catch the ball and pass it down the field. When close to the goal, they fling the ball to score points. The Wild Potato players aren't very aggressive. They push their way down the field, but they can't maintain the momentum to score. The Bird clan wins the game in less than two hours.

As the third game begins, Issaqueena slides in beside Bronco. He has given up on her. "I'm glad you came. I've been watching the game, and I have a few questions. The Deer clan is playing the Blue clan."

Issaqueena is pleased that he missed her. "Shad is playing for the Blue clan. I must warn you. Last year he actually won both games for his clan. He plays with total abandon and is notorious in his actions and deeds. I don't approve of the way he plays, but there are no rules to follow. We've had players like him before. Eventually Shad will compete against someone who equals his strength and cunning."

Bronco is surprised. "Well, someone got up on the wrong side of the bed this morning! You sound like a doomsday forecaster. Is his conduct on the field one of the reasons you dislike Shad?"

Issaqueena thinks for a few seconds before speaking, "It's not always my choice. There are some people I am required to tolerate. Shad is one of them. There's no one in this village I can tell except you."

"I'm honored you can talk to me, but why can you tell me and not someone else?"

"You are not Cherokee. You are not adopted by a clan. I asked that you be allowed to play for my clan. I know you're the person who can stand up to Shad. I've known that since the first time I met you. You will fulfill your destiny and then leave."

Bronco is shocked. "Are you saying you can tell what will happen in the future?"

"Yes. I didn't choose the gift of foresight. Mine is not an easy life. Today we work together to free my tribe of a detrimental element."

"I thought Shad was important to this tribe. Are you saying he's a hindrance to your tribe?"

"Everyone in my tribe thinks Shad is good for us, but I know what he'll do in the future if you don't take him out."

"Do you mean that I'll kill him today?"

Carefully she tells him, "You won't kill him today, but you'll learn to hate him. You'll kill him later. This is all I will say about his death."

"You have laid a heavy burden on my soul, Issaqueena. I don't know how to react. Will you be helping me in the future?"

"Yes, I'm an important part of your future. We'll watch this game together and begin our journey."

The third game of the day is the Blue clan and the Deer clan. Bronco and Issaqueena watch the game and study the techniques used by the warriors. They discuss how Bronco can counteract many of Shad's actions.

The game lasts for eight hours. The Blue clan finally reaches 12 pegs. The final score is 12 to 10. All the goals are two pointers.

Due to the length of the game, the Paint clan must wait until dawn to play the Wolf clan. Then the winner will play the Blue clan who will be rested and ready to win. Not the best scenario for Bronco and his fellow players who must play 2 games with no rest between.

Dawn comes quickly and the Paint clan faces the Wolf clan. Having the 'by' is a great advantage. This is the first game for Bronco and his fellow players. Bronco pairs off with a player his same height and build. As the game begins, Bronco races for the ball. He knocks several players out of his way. He catches the ball and flings it toward the goal. The ball connects with the post at a lower level. He scores the first two points. The players reassemble and a medicine man tosses the ball into play. Bronco races toward the ball. One of Bronco's clansmen used his wooden racket to knock out a Wolf clan warrior who happened to be Bronco's paired mate. Bronco has to leave the game, too. He doesn't like it, but it's the most important rule of the game.

Issaquena comes over to him. "You are really a great player. Don't worry. Our team will win and we'll face the Blue clan. Shad will be your hardest task. It's good that you can rest now. We have many players waiting for the final game. You are most important in the outcome of the next game, so you must be fresh and at your best."

Bronco waits impatiently for the final game. He speaks softly, "Thanks for the encouragement. I trust you. I'll rest."

Just as she foretold, the Paint clan wins. The final game will be the Paint clan and the Blue clan. Bronco doesn't know what to expect, but he is rested and alert.

Chapter 21

As the game begins, the first face he sees is Shad's. Shad has used excessive force by sweeping unsuspecting warriors off their feet and often delivering low blows to the base of the spine. He's taller than most of the players, and the shorter players learn to stay out of his way. Shad revels in his ability to hurt others.

Bronco whispers to Issaqueena, "I dislike bullies. I'll take Shad down, up close and personal."

Bronco runs onto the field and into danger. He pairs himself with Shad so he will be in the game as long as Shad. The clans assemble for the first toss of the game. Bronco catches the leather ball in the pouch of his racket. He tosses it to a member of his clan who catches it and passes it down the field. It is a team effort that pays off with 2 points.

As the teams reassemble, Bronco doesn't see Shad coming from the rear. He clips Bronco at the knees causing a domino effect which results in a stack of bodies.

"I should've been watching for that," Bronco tells himself. "Why would he treat me differently from anyone else? I won't underestimate him again."

After the clipping, Shad races for the goal, flings the ball, and scores the first points for the Blue clan.

The ball is tossed into play. Bronco doesn't hesitate. He lunges and connects. He catches Shad under the chin with his right elbow. Shad is surprised and stumbles backwards, but he regains his composure. A slow smile crosses his face as he winks at Bronco. The clash of the warriors has begun.

Shad springs to his feet and pursues the ball. Bronco waits for an opening. Shad catches the ball and flings it. Bronco jumps and intercepts the ball. He passes it to a teammate just as Shad hits him from the side. Bronco instinctively strikes Shad with a palm strike to the face. Shad rolls off and clasps his nose. Bronco doesn't wait for Shad to recover. He follows his Paint clan as they race down the field to score two points.

Shad recovers quickly. Bronco catches the toss and races toward the goal. Shad slams his racket on Bronco's forearm dislodging the ball from the stick. Shad scoops it up. Bronco doesn't hesitate. He breaks one of his rackets on the back of Shad's head. Shad stumbles but doesn't fall. He passes the ball to a fellow clan member who races down the field to score two more pegs.

As the next toss begins, Bronco looks for Shad, but he isn't visible. Out of nowhere, Shad appears and trips Bronco. Bronco jumps up and looks down the field. He smiles. "And let the fun begin!"

And it does. The action picks up and the blows become more violent. Bronco fights his way down the field and hurls the ball into the top of the goal for seven points. His team is now ahead nine to four.

The Blue clan claims the next toss and takes the ball down the field. Shad strikes Bronco across the face with his forearm. The blow causes Bronco to stumble and fall. A Blue clan warrior scoops up the ball and scores seven points to put them ahead eleven to nine.

Up to this point, Bronco has kept Shad from hurting others. All of Shad's attacks are centered on Bronco. Both teams race down the field. Bronco jabs the handle of his racket at the base of Shad's spine. Shad falls to the ground. He rises slowly. If Shad can't continue to play, then Bronco will be required to leave the field.

"Are you all right, Shad? I'm sorry, man. I didn't mean to hit you so hard."

"Don't worry about it. It's part of the game. I'll be fine. I just need a moment to catch my breath. Who scored?"

"My clan. The game is now tied eleven- eleven. The next team to score wins. I plan for that to be my clan."

"Over my dead body, Bear Man. Over my dead body."

Bronco remembers what Issaqueena said. "Not today, my friend. Not today."

The final toss is caught by the Blue clan and carried down the field. Each team has four players remaining. Bronco and Shad run side by side. Each is determined to win. The Paint clan retrieves the ball as Shad takes something out of a hole in the ground. Bronco dives at Shad's knees. Shad hits him on the head with the rock he has taken from the hole.

Bronco lies unconscious on the field. Shad should leave the field, but he doesn't. He races down the field in a rage. He uses his racket to cripple one Paint player. He attacks the next player with the same rock he used on Bronco. The remaining Paint player hurls the ball with all his strength and connects with the goal for two points and the victory. Shad is so angry he uses all his strength to backhand the victorious player. The Paint player falls lifeless to the ground.

Shad doesn't stop. He crosses the stream and heads north to his clan's village. Bronco regains consciousness just in time to witness the death of his clan member. He hasn't kept his clan safe from Shad. He blames himself for the death of this young brave.

Loving Woman stands on the sideline. Bronco goes over and takes her hands and walks her onto the field where her youngest son lies dead. He lifts the young warrior and yells as loud as he can, "Shad, I'm coming for you. You will be held responsible for this action."

CHAPTER 22

The Paint clan grieves the loss of Loving Woman's son. The death of a player can be accepted, but not this time. Shad knows the rules of the game. He should've left the field when Bronco was knocked out. Instead, he attacked the remaining players of the Paint clan. Shad is shunned and is no longer welcome in the Paint village.

Issaqueena stays closer to Bronco and becomes his interpreter. "Bear Man, the nights are getting much colder now. Your bedroll is no longer sufficient. It's time for you to make yourself a winter robe. What type robe do you have in mind?"

"After much thought, I have decided on bear. I don't remember hunting for bear. I guess that's part of the amnesia. But with your help, I'll have a bear robe before the snow falls."

He pauses before asking, "How do the Cherokee catch a bear? I'm open to suggestions."

"Most build bear traps. They use logs 8-10 inches diameter. They sharpen one end of the logs and drive them into the ground at different heights. Then, the top of the logs are sharpened. It takes about 12 stakes to form the back and sides. They prevent the bear from coming through the back to get the bait." She pauses. "Do you understand what to do so far?"

"Yes, I'm visualizing the placement of the logs."

"Then, you must tie a heavy log high in a tree. Attach the rope to the bait trap. It will release the heavy log so it falls on the bear and breaks its back. A bear is a very dangerous creature. Caution is necessary."

"Issaqueena, you make it seem so simple. When do we start?"

"We can go into the forest now and pick out some trees. I'll mark them; you cut them down. Have you ever handled an ax before?"

"I think I have." Bronco laughs. "We'll find out for sure when it's time to cut down a tree."

The two friends walk leisurely through the woods. They talk about the daily life of the Cherokee people. Issaqueena speaks of the broken peace treaties and the many hardships and disappointments suffered. Bronco begins to understand why the Indians hate the white man. Being a very empathetic person, Bronco experiences the pain of the Cherokee people and the shame of the white man.

"Why do your people continue to make treaties they know the white man won't honor?"

"You must understand. My people do not wish to fight. In the past, we believed treaties would be honored. We placed our trust in the wrong people. They didn't have the power to control the white man's greed. As more and more settlers entered our lands, we presented our concerns to the authorities. They were very receptive to our problems. We negotiated new treaties with the hope that someone in high places would enforce them. Other than the color of our skin, we're not so different from the white man. We live in homes, not caves. We hunt and fish. We raise our families to respect their elders. We live in villages much like your towns. Most of all, we seek peace."

"You said you could see the future. Have you seen the future of the Cherokee people?"

"Yes, I have, and it's not good. I will not discuss what I have seen with you. There's one thing certain. When outnumbered, defeat is inevitable."

"I fear you're correct. Bear Dog and I are going to scout the area. I'll be looking for bear tracks and a location for the trap. I'll mark the trees as I go, and I'll see you back in the village."

CHAPTER 23

The hills around Keowee are filled with game. Bronco sees many tracks, but none are bear tracks. He decides to travel south. He has strange feelings as he nears the river.

"I must have been here before. Look, Bear Dog. Several sets of small bear tracks. And, where there are small tracks, there should be large tracks close by."

"Oh, how I would love to kill the black mama bear that almost killed us. I'll build my trap here and hope for the best. Come, Bear Dog. Let's gather materials and return to build a strong bear trap."

The next morning the search for the perfect trees begins. Issaqueena has some duties to perform before she can help him.

"Well, Bear Dog, it's you and me ole boy. Let's get to work."

Bronco whispers as he reaches around for an ax. "Remember this whit rock we found along the bank of the river yesterday? I'm going to use it to sharpen this ax."

He comes to an abrupt stop. "How do I know I can sharpen an ax?" Bear Dog appears to understand what Bronco is saying. "Your guess is as good as mine. It's strange how I know some things and not others."

He and Bear Dog approach the trees he had marked for the back and sides of his trap.

Issaqueena walks up to them, "Good morning, Bear Man. Good morning Bear Dog. I managed to complete my business early. I can help you now."

A sigh of relief escapes, "I'm so glad to see you here. I really do need some help. I can handle the chopping if you help me guide the tree where I want it to fall. I won a tree chopping contest one time."

"What did you say? You won a tree chopping contest one time? Are you remembering something?"

"I don't know. I said it so it must be true. Do you think my memory is returning? Can isolated events return? I know I chopped a tree in a contest, and I won. This is scary."

"Bear Man, don't be afraid to remember. Relax and think about the contest. This could be what triggers your subconscious and returns your memory."

Bronco relaxes for several minutes, but nothing else breaks through.

"Let's get to work. Maybe the chopping will help me."

Issaqueena is all the help he needs. Together they cut down the chosen trees and drag them to the spot for his bear trap.

Bronco is so excited about their progress. "I can't believe how much we've done today. We are half way there. Tomorrow we'll cut them in half and sharpen them. I can make a pole driver to drive the logs. I've made them before."

"You've made them before? Perhaps you are a logger. That would explain your muscle development and muscle memory. You make chopping trees look simple. The repetitive movements are second nature to you."

He stops, "How do you know all these things? I thought you could see the future, not the past."

Issaqueena walks to Bronco and places her hands on his chest. "I am very good at reading people, and I want to help you."

Bronco places his hands on her hips and pulls her close. Isaqueena stands up on her toes. He kisses her lightly on the forehead. Then he slowly places feather like kisses on her eyes. He lifts her chin and covers her lips with a soft tender kiss. She moves closer and their bodies seem to merge. For several minutes they become as one. Their spirits rise above them and their souls unite. They belong to each other. They are truly soul mates. Issaqueena has waited for this man all her life.

This dynamic joining of their two souls takes Bronco by surprise. He jerks away. "What just happened here?"

"You discovered what I have known since my childhood. You and I were destined to meet, fall in love, and marry."

Bronco takes another step backwards. He looks at her carefully. "I'm trying to sort this out. I don't understand how this could be possible. I don't know who I am, but I know I'm not Cherokee. I know we can't be together until my memory returns. I don't want to hurt you. Maybe I should leave the village."

"No, Bear Man. You mustn't leave the village. It would be too dangerous for you. Promise me you won't leave."

"I promise I'll tell you when I decide to leave." A slow grin spreads across his face. "I'll not be leaving before winter, so we need to work a little harder to get me a bear skin."

The tension between them dissolves as they start back to the village. They plan to return at daybreak and get most of the trap finished. He hasn't found the strong, heavy log necessary to break the bear's back, but he is confident it will show up.

CHAPTER 24

The next morning is bright and clear. Issaqueena waits outside her hut. The sun rises behind her creating a golden glow. Bronco finds her beauty breathtaking. He nods his head, and she walks toward him. They fall into step as they walk down the path. They joke and play as companions. Onlookers could mistake them for an old married couple taking a morning walk.

Today they take a different route. As they near the place chosen for the trap, Bronco notices a huge tree limb that has fallen during the night.

He leads Issaqueena to the limb. "Look. This is exactly what we need to complete the trap."

Issaqueena looks confused. "There is no way the two of us can move that thing."

"Don't worry. Just give me a couple of ropes and I'll make a device we can use to move this log. Then we can use the ropes to place it up in a tree so it will fall on the bear and break its back, or at least it can trap the bear so I can kill it."

"You used ropes to help the women of my clan gather the corn quickly. How do you know about using ropes to move things that are very heavy?"

Bronco stops. "I did it again, didn't I? I remembered something from my past. Do you think I might be on the way to recovery?"

Issaqueena hesitates. "You will recover everything, but not without a loss. It will happen suddenly, and you will act without hesitation."

"How will this affect you? You said we'd marry."

"I said we'll marry, but I didn't say when. We'll have problems along the way, but we'll come together when least expected. This is all I know."

They reach the trees they felled the day before. Bronco cuts the trees in half and sharpens one end. It isn't long before they are ready to drive the trees.

Bronco picks up his tool bag. "Let me show you something I found last night. An old iron pot someone had thrown into the woods. I also found some old harnesses to add to the handles. I'll dig a trench. You can hold the log upright while I place the pot above the log. Then I'll jerk it down as hard as I can. This is how we drove the logs when they were over our heads."

"That makes sense. There is no way to use a mallet on logs this high. I'm impressed, Bear Man. You must have been very important to your town. You know how to make things that help with the difficult work."

"I'm not sure how important or how intelligent I am. The knowledge just appears in my mind."

They set all the back posts to keep the bear from taking the bait from the rear. Another log is set at the left front and one at the right front. These will hold the small logs for the bait. The trap requires the bear to enter from the front. When the bear grabs the bait, it will trip the rope that holds the heavy log. The heavy log will fall onto the bear.

With the trap completed and the bait set, the couple heads home. The nights are growing much colder. Fires and fireplaces are running full blast. Bronco has removed some of the rocks from the back of Isaqueena's fireplace. He's made a door at the back so ashes can be removed from the outside and not carried through the hut. He also has built a lean-to. He places it against the outside of the fireplace at night and sleeps in comfort. The villagers are amazed at how much warmth the shelter catches from the fireplace. When the temperature drops lower, the small door can be opened to give more heat to his structure. In the case of ice or snow, the shelter can be stored while the family moves into the sweat lodge. But, in any case, Bronco needs a robe to ward off the mountain's winter.

Bronco checks the trap several times a day. He and Bear Dog scout for a place to hide and safely watch the trap. They find a huge rock with an indention at ground level. Millions of years of erosion carved a place large enough for Bronco and Bear Dog to sit comfortably. The slight overhang cuts off most of the cold wind. There is no chance a bear can see or smell the pair.

A week later, Bronco and Bear Dog are in their hiding place. Bear Dog sits up as tall as he can and points his ears toward the trail. Bronco cautions the dog to remain silent. He can see the oncoming bear, a giant of a bear. His heart beats faster. The bear cautiously reaches for the bait. It taps the bait with its paw. The bait doesn't move. The bear looks around and sniffs the air. It turns and walks back about 50 feet.

Again, the bear watches for some movement. A few minutes later, its curiosity wins out. The bear walks back to the trap. This time it doesn't use its paw. The bear reaches for the bait with its mouth. It digs its sharp teeth in and pulls with all its might. The trigger releases the heavy log overhead. It falls across the back and shoulders of the bear, but it doesn't kill it. The log merely stuns it. The bear begins to flail its arms and dig with its back feet. The giant log does not budge. It has wedged in the opening between the back logs and the front log on the left.

Bronco and Bear Dog move quietly. Bear Dog circles around the bear and waits for Bronco to advance. Brandishing the large ax he has made for chopping the logs, Bronco swings around with an upward chop. He drives the ax head into the soft spot just below the bear's throat.

The bear howls and struggles, but Bronco pulls upward with all his might. The ax head destroys the bear's throat. The howling stops and the bear falls forward. The giant is dead. Bronco rolls the log off the beast's back. He manages to turn the bear enough to retrieve his ax. He is thrilled. His rug will be large enough to envelop both he and Bear Dog on the cold winter nights ahead.

"Bear Dog, go to the village. Find Issaqueena. She'll know I have killed a bear. She'll bring some braves to help us carry it to the village. I'll field dress the bear while you're gone."

In less than an hour, Issaqueena and some braves arrive.

"Bronco, when I saw Bear Dog, I knew you had killed a large bear and needed help to carry it." Her eyes almost pop out of her head. "I'm glad we brought a carrier with us."

Everyone is excited. The braves are talking and laughing in their native tongue. They shake Bronco's hand and pat him on the back.

Issaqueena hugs Bronco, "This is the largest bear ever killed by a member of my clan. The bear meat is desperately needed to feed our village this winter. It is understood that the hide belongs to you, but the food will be shared with the village. Is that correct?"

Bronco continues to hold her as he spoke. "I wouldn't have it any other way. I'm sure this bear will weigh between 500 and 600 pounds, and I'm more than pleased to help feed the village this winter. There's only one problem. Do you think this carrier is strong enough to get this giant to the village?"

Bronco and Issaqueena laugh. Some of the braves know enough English to recognize that Bronco is proud to share with them, and he is joking about the carrier. They laugh with him.

One of the braves speaks in broken English. "Your bear very large. It take us all pull him to village."

There is much laughing and playful joking. A family atmosphere hangs over the group and makes the difficult task pass quickly.

CHAPTER 25

As the group tops the hill that overlooks the village, the braves begin to whoop and holler. Everyone in the village knows that something great has happened. They rush to meet the group. The people recognize this as the biggest bear ever killed by a member of their village.

The women are both thrilled and excited. They race to their huts for their knives and cleaning implements.

Bronco is amazed at what he sees. "I don't believe my eyes. The women are so organized. They're ready to work. The braves know exactly where to put the bear and how to help the women start."

"Watch closely, Bear Man. You haven't seen how this machine works, yet. The women are very careful. They will not damage the hide. First, the bear will be cut open and the insides will be removed. Nothing will be wasted. The stomach will be used as a water bag. The intestines will be stuffed with prepared bear meat. The women will prepare the liver and serve it to you and the braves who helped bring the bear here. The heart is yours. The heart contains the spirit of the bear. By eating the heart, you'll absorb the strength and characteristics of the animal."

Bronco watches, "As soon as they finish, I plan to tan the whole hide. What do I do first?"

"The village has a large boiling pot. I'll help you mix alum, salt, crushed hickory bark, and water. The hide must soak 24 hours to set the hair. The village has some extra stretching racks. We must scrape all the fat off the hide or it will turn rank and draw flies and bugs. When thoroughly dried and cured, we'll rub some of this oil to soften the hide. All this will take several weeks."

Bronco laughs, "I will freeze to death before then."

Issaqueena smiles, "I won't allow you to freeze. You may sleep in the sweat lodge. I have always heard the white man is soft. If you freeze to death, then you'll be proving what I've always heard."

"This bear hide will keep me warm for a long time. Let's get started."

They move to the working station. The inner organs and the meat have been removed. The bear is a female. Bronco studies the hide carefully. He checks the inside of the neck. "HEY! Look at this! These marks indicate that something bit deeply into the neck and held on."

He looks a little closer. "I think this is the mama bear that attacked me. The marks on the neck could be Bear Dog's teeth prints. He latched onto the bear and refused to let go. Shad said he heard the bear roar as he fought with Bear Dog. The bear knocked me over the cliff. That was when Bear Dog released his hold on the bear and dove into the water after me. This makes the bear very important to me. I can certainly say revenge is sweet, don't you think?"

"Yes, I do. Come, let's get this bad boy into the pot."

After several weeks, the hide is finally ready to be rubbed with bear oil. This takes a little more time. Bronco waits impatiently.

When it's complete, Bronco parades around the camp in his new hide. The bear robe is large enough to cover Bronco and hangs just below his knees. The villagers applaud and cheer loudly.

Issaqueena turns to her father. "It is truly a magnificent hide worn by a magnificent man." Her father doesn't like the look on her face as she watches the white man win the hearts of her people.

Snow flakes begin to fall as Bronco returns to Issaqueena's side. "We finished this robe just in time. The sweat lodge is warm, but this robe will make it even more comfortable."

"If this snow continues and the temperature drops, my father and I will be in the sweat lodge with you."

Bronco winks, "Come on in. The more the merrier. My robe is large enough for us both."

Issaqueena blushes as she looks into his face. She dreads the day his memory returns. She knows he will leave her and return to his family and friends.

CHAPTER 26

It is January 1760, and snow covers the ground. Most of the people stay inside their huts or their sweat lodges. Very little socializing occurs; so, it comes as a surprise when the elders call a meeting in the Council House.

Bronco isn't allowed inside, but this hasn't stopped him before. In fact, the villagers have been told not to speak the Cherokee language when Bear Man is near. Issaqueena doesn't want him to understand the Cherokee language. Yet, over the months, he has eavesdropped and learned many of the words. He hasn't let them know that he can understand what they say. He sits outside at the back of the Council House where he can listen and not be found.

All of the clans are well represented except the Blue clan. Their section is noticeably empty. The topic of this meeting is the Blue clan who has been attacking settlers without consulting the Council.

War Eagle, the leader of the Paint clan, speaks against the Blue clan. "I do not feel we should be attacking settlers at this time. We must contact the white father in Washington and let him know the settlers are breaking the treaty. I fear the Blue clan's actions will negate the treaty, and we'll lose more of our land. They endanger the whole Cherokee tribe. A new war may begin because of their actions."

Issaqueena speaks, "It is rumored the Blue clan will raid the French Huguenot camp near the river called Long Cane. We know the Blue clan has white man weapons far superior to ours. It was Shad who helped his clan steal the weapons from 96. I believe Shad is responsible for the recent raids."

When Bronco hears that Shad stole the weapons and supplies from 96, he remembers who he is and where he lives. Somehow he knows that Shad is at the bottom of all this. He stole the supplies to use against the settlers. Bronco returns to the sweat lodge and curls up in his bear skin. Shad was his friend until he killed Loving Woman's son. Bronco knows the time has come for him to rid the Cherokee of Shad and his hate of white people.

When Issaqueena finds him, she doesn't speak. She knows something is wrong. She fears his memory is returning. If the clan finds out, Bear Man could be put to death. When Shad brought him to the village, Issaqueena promised to be responsible if Bronco caused any harm to the tribe. She must help Bronco, the man of her future.

The next morning brings another day of white gloom. The snow cripples the village.

Bear Man approaches the fire. Issaqueena sees Bronco's face and knows he will leave soon.

He voices exactly what she is thinking. "I have to leave this village. I'm needed in 96 to protect my family and friends from the renegade clan. Did I understand Shad and his clan have attacked settlers in this area?"

"Yes, they've been graphic in the murders. They have dismembered, tortured, and even scalped the victims. Men, women, and children have been slaughtered. I fear the wrath of the white man. He won't care that we have nothing to do with the attacks. One clan's actions affect us all. This is exactly what the white man wants. He'll step in now and punish us all. He'll take the best of our lands and leave us with the part no white man wants."

"I'm so sorry, Issaqueena." Bronco takes her in his arms and lets her cry for all things the Indians will lose. "But I need you to understand why I must leave. My family and my friends are in danger. If we are to be together, we'll find each other again. I must leave now before your people discover I have regained my memory. I'm no longer safe here."

"Bear Man, I have always known you would go back to your family. I have tried to make the most of the time we've had together. You must leave quickly. We'll meet again in the future. Watch for me. I will come to you."

Issaqueena gives Bronco her fastest horse. He must get as far away as possible before someone realizes he's gone.

It is unthinkable to journey far from the village in this weather, but the Blue clan is attacking all the settlers they find on the disputed land. Bronco's first stop is Long Cane Village where he left Michael. He hopes he isn't too late.

CHAPTER 27

It is February 1, 1760. Several months have passed since Bronco left Michael with the French Huguenots at the village on Long Cane Creek. Michael has watched for Bronco's return, but he's almost forgotten Bronco and the town of 96. After a few months he has become an integral part of the community.

Michael and Renee are engaged. The bans have been posted, and a date is set. The young couple walks along the familiar path to the waterfall where Michael broke his leg.

Michael turns to Renee, "I've been here for 6 months. I have no real family in 96, and if I never return, no one will miss me. I did odd jobs around town and slept in the stable. I've decided I'll stay here with you. I would never ask you to leave your family."

Renee looks into his face. "I'm glad you feel at home here. I don't want to leave, but I would go with you to 96." She looks at the landscape with new appreciation. "It's time for the snows to fall."

Joking, Michael grinned, "Perhaps we could marry now so we can keep each other warm this winter. I'm sure the men will help us build a small house and a barn. I'd like to marry you before you change your mind."

They laugh. "I can't believe how lucky I am. I break a leg and meet the girl of my dreams. Who would guess?"

"Not me," Renee is adamant. "I'd doubt your honesty with a story like that."

They are admiring the waterfalls when a young man suddenly appears. He yells, "I need some help. Help me, please." They race to the foot of the falls.

The young man cries out, "My village is not far from here. The Cherokee overtook my family's farm two days ago. The Indians are still camped at the edge of our village. I don't know why they are staying. There's nothing left for them. I'm afraid they'll hit your village next."

Michael supports the exhausted young man. "Let's get you back to our village. There's always something over the fire for a hungry person. I want you to tell the others what you just told me. They'll decide if we fight, or if we run."

The young man pleads, "The smartest thing to do is run. My people decided to fight. They really thought they could defeat a tribe of trained warriors. It was the wrong choice. I was sent to warn you. I don't know if anyone else escaped. I hope to find my family, but they are most certainly dead."

Michael and Renee help the young man to the camp. They give him some food and bring the elders to listen to what he has to say.

Everyone listens intently. Renee's father Pierre speaks up. "I know it sounds like the cowardly thing to do, but we should load up the wagons with minimal supplies and run. We can travel to 96 and warn them just as this young man has warned us. Let's not make the same mistake as his village."

Michael speaks up. "I can lead you to 96. I know a shorter way."

They agree and load the wagons quickly. They are in a hurry to leave. They are only a short distance from the village when the band of Cherokee warriors attack.

Michael is shocked at what he sees. A large black man is leading the renegade warriors. He wears war paint and waves a long rifle. He's obviously in command.

He turns to Renee and whispers. "We're in for a real battle. The guy at the front is the one I told you about. He stole our guns and ammo. We were following him to regain our supplies."

Michael yells, "Shad, is that you?"

The leader turns and shots a wicked glance at Michael.

Michael cringes as Shad stares him down. "I wonder what he's done with Bronco."

The Frenchmen have never fought Indians; so, Michael takes over and begins giving instructions. "Stay under or behind your wagons. Stay hidden. We must not get out in the open. It will be easier if the

Indians come to us. We have the advantage. They didn't expect to find us prepared for their attack. They expected to surprise us in the village. We may be able to chase them away."

100 angry warriors rush the wagons again and again. Some of their horses drop from fatigue. The warriors continue to rush and retreat. The Huguenots foil the braves' strategy by not taking chase. Between the advances, the settlers care for their wounded and grieve for those who are taken prisoner.

For several hours the settlers defend their wagons. It is a sad day for the Huguenots. 150 settlers leave the village. 23 die before the attackers' final retreat into the woods.

Of the 75 adults and 40 male defenders, the children are the most vulnerable. Several children are slain and scalped. A few of the children are taken prisoner.

Michael again asks for immediate action, "I know you value family and friends, but we don't have time to grieve or bury the dead. We must dig a mass grave for the fallen. Then we'll run before the Cherokee regroups and attacks again."

Pierre agrees. "It sounds heartless, but I agree with Michael. We must run for our lives. Our dead would expect nothing more than what we're doing. They would tell us to save the remaining villagers. We'll dig deep enough to prevent the ravaging of wild animals, but we must hurry. Let's get to work."

They dig a shallow mass grave for the twenty-three who lie dead. There is no time for a ceremony. They climb into their wagons and ask their horses to move faster than ever before.

The Cherokee expect the villagers to camp overnight and bury their dead according to customs. After sunset the braves retrieve their dead and wounded. The total is 21 killed or wounded. They are surprised the next morning to find all the wagons gone.

The Huguenots push their horses to the point of exhaustion. They dare not stop for any length of time. They stop only to water the horses. Pemmican and jerky are passed from wagon to wagon. No one complains. No children cry. They are all of the same mindset—escape.

It is becoming too dark for them to travel. The horses stumble and need rest more than the villagers do. Yet, there is hope; no warriors are in sight.

Shortly after sundown, they reach the settlement of Due West. The villagers welcome them with open arms. When they hear about the uprising, they become fearful.

Michael pleads, "The Cherokee are right behind us. Come with us to 96. There is a stockade-fort there. It is so much easier to defend. It offers sanctuary to all who need protection from the Indians. Please, come with us."

Jonathan reinforces Michael's plea. "You know that I'm from 96. I assure you Michael speaks the truth. The fort is a stronghold. It would be best for all of us if we travel with the group to 96."

Several of the families work all night loading their wagons. Just before sunrise Michael makes one last plea. "I hope you've made the right decision. We lost twenty-three men, women, and children yesterday. We would have lost more had we stayed to fight. We are not trained Indian fighters. We are farmers with families. Please reconsider. Our trail won't be hard to follow."

Michael turns to his followers. "We should arrive at 96 before sunset. Let's head out. Goodbye and good luck. You'll need it."

CHAPTER 28

Just as Michael promised, they travel fast and arrive in 96 before sunset. Everyone he remembers is there to greet them. It is a happy reunion until William Manley asks about Bronco.

Michael explains, "We were separated after I broke my leg at Long Cane Village. I stayed there to heal. After a few months, I thought Bronco must have caught up with Shad, and something bad must've happened. I didn't give up hope, but I knew he would've been in contact with us if he could. Now the Indians are attacking settlers."

No sooner than it is out of Michael's mouth, a lone rider comes into view. It is Bronco. His mom and his dad race out of the fort to meet him.

Patricia begins to cry. "Where have you been, son? We've been so worried about you. Let me look you over. You look like my Bronco. Say something so I'll know it's really you."

"Well, mom," Bronco rattles off an explanation just like when he was a young boy. "I was injured and suffered amnesia. My memory returned two days ago. Since then I've been tracking the renegade warriors who are destroying every village they can find. Long Cane Village is burned to the ground. I could tell the French Huguenots had been warned. They had loaded their wagons and left. I saw a mass grave a few miles from Long Cane."

Bronco pauses and realizes his mom's eyes are open in horror and disbelief. "Mom, I just gave you the highlights. Did I talk too fast?"

Patricia hugs his neck. "Son, when you're ready to tell us in a slower form, we'll listen. I can't follow your rapid, condensed version just now."

William arrives and sees that Patricia has found their son. "Bronco, you may think you're a grown man, but I'll never again let you go anywhere without me. What's going on with the Indians?"

"The Cherokee warriors of the Blue clan are attacking settlers all along the Cherokee Trail. They aren't sparing anyone. They are murdering men, women, and children. They're on their way here. We have no time to spare. We need to get everyone into the fort and ready for the attack."

William turns to the refugees, "Let's put the horses in the stable. The wagons can stay outside the compound. If you brought any supplies with you, get them from the wagons now. We have food and blankets we can share. It's going to be crowded, but we'll manage."

Bronco addresses the Lone Cane group. "It's been two days since you were attacked. You're safe here. The fort was designed for this purpose. Michael, you and Jonathan climb to the top of the ammo shed. You'll be able to spot the braves before they come out of the woods. Mr. Brown, please divide the ammo and place it at each point of our star. We must expect attack from any, if not all, angles. The braves are strong and highly trained in combat. Shoot to kill. Don't play with them. We can't let them get over the wall."

Everything is in place when Bronco speaks again. "We'll be on the buddy system. The person next to you is your buddy. Decide which of you will take the first watch. It's up to the individuals how long one of the pair sleeps. We must be on guard. You've never fought anyone like the Cherokee warrior. Don't give him an inch. If they're close enough to the fort, fire your weapon. I repeat. Shoot to kill."

Jonathan is somewhat confused by Bronco's orders. "It's only a couple of hours until sunset. I've heard they don't attack after dark."

Bronco emphasizes, "Don't put anything past them. We'll remain on guard throughout the night. Take nothing for granted. They are relentless fighters. Once a battle begins, they fight until they win or lose. Never underestimate your opponent."

Michael yells from atop the ammo shed. "I see something moving along the wood line. It might be human. I'll keep a watch and tell you when I'm sure of what it is."

"Thanks, Michael. You're still my right-hand man. Welcome back."

"Bronco, I'm seeing movement back and forth. It might be an animal-- a dog. Could it be that the braves are trying to draw us out?"

"Michael, I'm coming up there." When Bronco reaches the top of the building, he can see the shape Michael questions. "I'm going just outside the barriers and see for myself."

Patricia becomes frantic. "Please, son, don't go outside the fort. You've just returned. I don't want to lose you again."

"Mom, don't worry. If it's what I think it is, we need it."

Bronco steps just outside the gate. He looks toward the woods and whistles. Cautiously the shadow moves toward the fort. "Bear Dog, is that you?"

The shadow becomes alert and points its ears toward the fort. "Bear Dog, it's OK. Come!" The dog walks slowly; still not sure Bronco is there."

Bear Dog walks up to Bronco and stands at his side scanning the woods for movement. Neither the man nor the dog shows emotion at this reunion. The people in the fort are surprised at this action and wonder what kind of relationship they have.

They walk through the gate together, the magnificent man and his trusted dog.

Patricia watches the dog and knows it's an important part of Bronco's recent time in the North. "Does this dog belong to you, Bronco?"

"It's more like I belong to him, mom. It's a long story which you'll love. I'll fill you in when we have more time. Right now, just know this dog is important to me."

"Would it be all right if I get him something to eat?"

"Well, mom, I see nothing has changed here. You are still worrying about someone going hungry. Feel free to bring him some food. I'm not sure he'll eat it. He usually finds his own food, but he occasionally accepts food from me. Give it a try, mom. Everyone loves you. Why would a dog be any different?"

Patricia returns with some meat from the supper. She approaches Bear Dog slowly. She offers the food. He sniffs both her and the food. Then he begins to eat the food she offers.

"Bronco, why do I get a strange feeling this dog can be dangerous?"

"That's because he is dangerous when he needs to be. Later, I'll tell you how he saved my life."

"You bet you'll tell me the whole story, young man. If this dog saved your life, then he's a member of our family, and I'll take care of him, too."

He places his arm on his mom's shoulder and laughs. "You are still the mom I know and love. You never change."

Bear Dog gives a low warning growl.

Bronco announces, "Alert, folks. There might be some company nearby. Watch carefully and don't drop your guard."

A few short minutes later, a flaming arrow comes over the wall. Once again the Indians use the attack/retreat tactic. It is not successful. The men and women in the fort watch intently and fire at anything that moves.

For two hours both forces square off. The Indians can't reach the fort. It's unlike them to give up. But they have failed with the Huguenots, and now they can't reach the fort. Two of their own lie dead. They recover the bodies and leave. They will rework their strategies and return.

Everyone breathes a sigh of relief when the Cherokee retreat. No more attacks. Now there is time for a family reunion.

Patricia asks, "What happened to you to make you so pale? You don't look as healthy as I remember."

"Mom, I was attacked by a large black bear. Had it not been for Bear Dog, I would be dead. First, he jumped on the bear's back and dug his teeth into the neck. When the bear knocked me over a cliff into a raging river, Bear Dog let go of the bear and dove in after me. He grabbed the neck of my buckskin shirt and kept my head above the water. I have no idea where he came from nor where he was headed. I was just lucky he was there."

"Son," Patricia is shocked. "Are you saying that this dog saved you from a bear?"

"Yes, and then we went over a waterfall."

Patricia places her hands on her face. "Oh! No! This just keeps getting better and better."

"Then, Bear Dog pulled me to the shore where Shad was waiting. At first, he wouldn't let Shad touch me. I had some severe wounds from the bear attack. I also had head injuries from the river and waterfall. Bear Dog finally let Shad help me along the path. But when I awoke, I couldn't remember who I was or where I was going. Shad couldn't carry me, so he went to a nearby Cherokee village and brought back several braves."

William places his hand on Bronco's shoulder. "Why didn't Shad kill you?"

"Shad was very afraid of Bear Dog. When he realized I had amnesia and was no longer a threat, he took me to the Paint clan because of their healer. She is called Issaqueena. She's a gifted healer and psychic. She's the reason I'm here today. I hated to leave her, but my memories returned. She understood I was needed here in 96."

Michael walks over to the group. "Bronco, I saw Shad leading the renegades. You said he went for help. Didn't he want you dead?"

"Yes, he did, so he stayed very close. In fact, he became my best friend. The Cherokee didn't speak in their native tongue when I was around. Shad was my interpreter. He answered my questions and taught me what I needed to survive in the Cherokee world. I really liked him until he killed a member of my clan. I hope to meet him again. He'll regret sparing my life."

Jonathan was listening nearby. He interrupts, "Did you find out where Shad took the weapons he stole from us?"

"I haven't seen any of our weapons until now. Some of our attackers were using our rifles and pistols. The Paint clan didn't know that Shad had our weapons. The Blue clan had been planning this war for quite some time."

CHAPTER 29

Issaqueena is very upset with Shad and the Blue Clan. She turns to her father, War Eagle, for some answers. "The Blue clan failed to defeat the French Huguenots at Long Cane, and now the fort at 96 has proven to be strong and impenetrable. The Blue clan has disgraced itself. Their return to Keowee will not be a welcome one."

War Eagle agrees with her. "An emergency meeting of the clans has been called. The other clans are as angry as we are. The Council will decide the fate for breaking the treaty and attacking white settlers."

Issaqueena continues to probe War Eagle for some answers. "The Tribal Council has forbidden the clans to attack settlers. Now the peace treaty is broken. The Blue clan's actions jeopardize our existence."

"Issaqueena, I agree with you, but I'm sure it will fall upon deaf ears. Shad and his followers are preparing for a return to 96 to destroy the occupants of the fort. Shad is obsessed with the fort's destruction." War Eagle walks away as if he is already defeated.

Issaqueena calls after War Eagle. "Shad won't stop until he's either dead or completes his vendetta against Bear Man and the residents of 96."

She is afraid Shad could succeed in killing the man she loves. She waits until the village is quiet and the members of her clan are sleeping. She speaks quietly to her horse. "Scout, my beloved horse, Bear Man and his people are in big trouble. You must help me get word to him as quickly as we can. I'll do my best not to overburden you, but, we must hurry or Bronco will die."

She quietly leads her horse to the edge of the village before mounting. She must stay ahead of Shad and the Blue clan.

She carries no food and no water. She goes around the Cherokee village located 6 miles from Keowee. She stops at every stream and calls it by the number of miles from her home. She stops at 12 mile creek, 18 mile creek, 20 mile creek, Three and Twenty Creek, and Six and Twenty Creek. She forages for berries and other edible roots at each creek. She makes sure her horse has plenty of water to drink and something to eat.

She talks to her horse. "Scout, I'm trying to take care of you. I'm asking for all your strength and courage. Together we'll succeed. The night's beautiful and the moon's full. Let's go just a little further before we stop for a nap."

After traveling for more than 15 hours, Isaqueena and Scout stop for more than water and food. They need to rest. They are so weary they sleep for several hours. When Issaqueena awakes, she climbs on her horse and heads toward Bronco and 96.

Issaqueena keeps her mind alert by talking to her horse. "I've traveled this trail several times. I know many traders between Keowee and Charles Town. One time I traveled to Augusta for some supplies I needed for my healing treatments."

Both Isaqueena and Scout are taxed to their limits. She studies the surrounding area. "Look, Scout. I know these are the remains of the Long Cane Village. Shad and his followers must have burned all the homes and barns before returning to Keowee. I'm sure they were quite frustrated with their failure to capture 96. It will be bad when Shad and Bear Man meet again."

The final miles are indeed the longest miles. Issaqueena and Scout move slowly as they approach a makeshift village on a creek where flakes of gold have been found. "Scout, you and I are very lucky that gold is not important to us. Shad must have attacked this small group. He shows no mercy. I don't know what made Shad hate white men so much. He brought Bear Man to our village because he needed to keep an eye on him. When I realized that Bear Man was in my future, I couldn't allow Shad to kill him."

A few hours later, Issaqueena sees a small sign: 96 Settlement-10 miles. She stops at the sign and begins to cry from exhaustion. "Oh, Scout, I can't believe we're almost there. This has been such a long, arduous journey. I couldn't have made it this far without you. If it's true that home is where the heart is, then we're almost home. Just 10 more miles, and we'll be with Bear Man."

She continues to push herself and her horse until she sees a clearing up ahead.

"Could this be the fort at 96? I'm not sure how we should approach. I'm sure there must be some guards on the wall. Oh, I can tie one of my leggings to this broken tree limb and use it as a flag of surrender. Bear Man is close; I can feel him."

Since Bronco's return, the villagers have looked to him for guidance. He has learned much while living with the Cherokee. He knows they will return full force, but he doesn't know when. He anticipates 100 or more warriors this time. As long as Shad and his group are kept outside, the people within the fort are safe. Hand-to-hand combat is the Cherokee's advantage.

Since Bronco's return, the men of the village have dug the outside trench deeper making it more difficult for the warriors to make it past the wall. They also fortified the ammunition shed so fire arrows won't cause any problems.

Bronco has explained to the settlers how the Indians use traps. The most dramatic is when they send in slaves or captives dressed in warlike costumes. Michael and Jonathon are instructed to call Bronco who will make the call to fire or not.

The women replenish the food shelves and bring in more plates and tableware to accommodate the visitors. Even in the midst of a crisis, the women try to uphold the laws of etiquette.

Issaqueena stands at the edge of the woods and observes the fort for a few moments. She climbs aboard Scout and they slowly walk out of the woods. She waves the legging and hopes someone will see her and motion her into the fort.

Jonathan is on top of the ammunition building when he spots a horse approaching. The rider is waving a flag of surrender. Can this be one of the traps?

"Bronco," yelled Jonathan, "there is a rider approaching waving a flag."

Bronco sprints to the shed and climbs to the top. He can see someone approaching. Bear Dog goes to the gate and begins to bark. He never barks. The villagers have heard him growl when something is wrong, but they have never heard him bark. Bronco doesn't know if Bear Dog is afraid or if he recognizes the rider's scent.

Bronco jumps from the roof of the shed. He flings open the fort's gate, and he and Bear Dog race out to meet the rider. The rider falls into Bronco's arms and begins to weep. He lifts her and carries her into the fort. Both Bear Dog and Scout follow the couple.

William and Patricia meet them at the gate. "Bronco, who is this woman?"

"She is the medicine woman who saved my life. She says that Shad and his follower's are on their way, just hours behind her. Dad, pull everyone together and tell them to prepare for attack. They know what their duties are. Jonathon, please be sure her horse is cared for. They have come a long way to warn us."

He carries Issaqueena into the guard house so she can rest. He holds her hand and listens to her talk about the council meeting and the Blue clan. She finally relaxes and drifts off to sleep.

"Bear Dog, stay here with her. If she wakes, she'll see you and know that everything is OK." He kisses her forehead and leaves the room.

Patricia is waiting outside the shed. Bronco hugs her neck. "It has been less than one month since Shad led the braves against the fort. Now it's only hours before he and his followers try again. I hope we're ready for them."

As he climbs to the top of the ammo shed, he glances at the wood line. The renegade clan has increased in size. The Indians number over 200 this time. His feeling of dread increases. He spots Shad at the center of the group.

Fire arrows flood into the fort, but the settlers are prepared. They know their jobs and fall into action. Nothing catches fire. Just like last time, a group of warriors race toward the fort only to be turned back by gunfire. The Indians begin to fire over the heads of their fellow tribesmen. They are using the stolen weapons. Several injuries occur on both sides.

Although weapons have been added as a new approach to the hit-and-run technique, not one of the warriors makes it to the log wall surrounding the fort. The stockade-fort withstands the constant 36 hour assault. Only two people inside the fort are injured. The Indian casualties are unknown. The Cherokee warriors are enraged at their inability to take over the fort. They leave 96 and ambush all the white people they can find along the trails of the backcountry.

CHAPTER 30

A strange feeling comes over Bronco. The hair on the back of his neck is standing up. He turns and sees Shad standing at the entrance of the covered passageway.

Shad steps into the sunlight. Bronco speaks first, "I should have remembered the passageway. I underestimated you."

"Yes, you did. And now, it's time for the showdown. I've wanted you dead for a long time. The time I spent here with your family and friends made me realize that you have everything I ever wanted. Your

parents and everyone in this village loves you. They talked about you all the time. I know it was jealousy on my part, but I resented the way you always won. I thought my chance had come when you caught up with me along the river. But the angry mama bear found you first. She slashed both of your arms before that devil dog jumped on her back and latched onto her neck. She was furious."

"Did you think the bear would do your dirty work for you?"

"You bet I did. She was swinging her paws with great force. She knocked you down while trying to rid herself of the dog. When she couldn't shake the dog, she struck at you again. She slapped you so hard that you went over the cliff and into the river below."

Shad pauses. He can see that Bronco is reliving the incident. "I've never seen anything like it. Bear Dog released that bear and dove over the cliff after you. I ran along the river and watched. That dog was amazing. He grabbed your buckskin shirt and kept your head above the water until you reached the waterfall. The dog lost his grasp on your shirt as you fell over the falls. I watched that dog swim to you and pull you to the shore. It was a thing of beauty."

He continues to gnaw at Bronco's pain in reliving the event. "Bear Dog wouldn't let me near you. He growled and he watched my every move. After what I saw him do, I wasn't going to mess with him. I had sent all the stolen weapons ahead with my crew. The only thing I had was a small knife. There was no way I could kill you both, and I feared I would be killed by whichever of you survived."

"Why didn't you kill me after we arrived in the village?"

"That was when I realized you had amnesia and was no longer a threat. When I took you to Issaqueena, she knew exactly what to do.

She healed you, and then you became everyone's favorite again. You helped the women harvest an abundant crop of corn. You killed the biggest bear the village had ever seen. You supplied the meat that would feed the village all winter. You almost killed me in the stickball game. Everyone loved you. Why couldn't they love me like that? What's wrong with me?"

"Shad, we were close friends until the games. If you hated me so much, why didn't you just kill me?"

"I have loved Issaqueena for a very long time. I used you as an excuse to be around her. She bossed me around like I was a slave. I am a freeman, not a slave. I wanted her to love me, but she fell in love with you, not me. I knew she asked you to control me during the game. She wanted you to keep me from hurting anyone. I took great joy in hurting you in the game, but I knew the only way to hurt you was by hurting someone you cared about. After I killed Loving Woman's son, they say you took an oath to kill me. Well, guess what. Today is your day."

Shad leaps. Bronco steps to the side. Shad can't stop. His weight pushes him forward. He regains his poise and turns. This time he waits.

He doesn't have long to wait. Bronco draws a knife and throws it. Shad tries to move out of the way, but he is too slow. The knife enters Shad's right thigh. He winces with pain, but he doesn't drop his guard. He pulls the knife out of his leg and throws it at Bronco who steps out of the way. As Bronco lunges forward, his tremendous fist catches Chad square on the jaw. Shad stumbles backwards, but he doesn't fall. He recovers and steps forward to grasp Bronco's shoulders. Shad laughs as he head-butts his opponent, but Bronco's head is like a piece of granite. Shad almost knocks himself out.

As Shad falters, Bronco punches him in the abdomen and follows with an uppercut to the chin. Shad is still standing. Bronco dives at Shad and takes him to the ground where he lands several blows to Shad's head. Shad rolls over and attempts to stand up with Bronco on his back.

Michael and Jonathan haven't seen the whole fight. They arrive just as Shad is up on his knees. They watch as Bronco continues Shad's momentum and lifts him up into the air. He bounces Shad on his shoulder and body slams him with tremendous force. With his knee in the center of Shad's back, Bronco snaps his neck.

He addresses the dead man, "You were right, my friend. Today is my day."

Michael runs up to Bronco, "Are you all right? How did Shad get inside the fort?"

Jonathan interrupts, "Is Shad dead?"

"Whoa! One question at a time, guys."

Michael sees that Bronco is exhausted but OK. He asks again, "How did Shad get inside the fort?"

"He found our weak spot. He came through the covered passageway from the village. We'll take care of that later. Right now, you guys take Shad's body and bury it somewhere. I don't want to know where. I'd like to forget I ever knew him."

Bronco walks away and leaves the boys with their assignment. He needs to see Issaqueena. They must decide where they go from here.

CHAPTER 31

Bronco was unable to stay at Isaqueena's side. He was the only person in the fort who knew how the Cherokee fight. He checked on Issaquena several times during the battle.

The first time Issaquena woke, she was confused. The strange ceiling over her head frightened her. She couldn't remember where she was or why she was there. Bear Dog nudged her hand with his head. Issaqueena reached out and hugged his neck. "Bear Dog! I'm so glad to see you. I know Bear Man is OK because you're here."

"Issaqueena," Patricia spoke softly. "Do you remember me? I'm Patricia Manley, Bronco's mom." Issaqueena still looked confused. Patricia explained, "I think you know my son as Bear Man."

"Yes, I know your son as Bear Man. He is a good man. You and your husband taught him well. I am lucky to know him."

Suddenly, the battle noises increased. Issaqueena was very frightened. "How long have I been asleep? Has Shad arrived with his clansmen? Is anyone in your village harmed?"

"Slow down, Issaqueena," Patricia takes her hand. "Everything's fine. The battle continues, but we are safe in the storage shed. Bronco has been in to see you several times. I promised him that I would take care of you. I have some water and something for you to eat. Then, I think you should try to rest some more. You have over taxed yourself."

Issaqueena ate what Patricia gave her. She did not realize how very tired she was. Even with the noise from the battle, she drifted off to sleep. Patricia never left her side. Each time Issaqueena woke, Patricia had something for her to eat or to drink.

Just before the end of the battle, Issaqueena became more alert and began to ask questions.

Patricia answered honestly. "Shad is dead, and all of the warriors have left the area. Everyone inside the fort is safe, especially you. I'm not sure how many of your tribe is dead or wounded. Bronco watched the braves retrieve their brothers from the open field."

Issaqueena sighs, "My people are so enraged. I fear they'll ambush and kill all the white people they can find. They will seek out every camp and village in the backcountry and destroy them all."

"You gave up your life and your family to warn us of the attack. You sacrificed everything to save us. Why did you do this?"

Issaqueena thinks for a few seconds and looks deep into Patricia's eyes. "I have loved your son since the first time I saw him. Nothing was more important than keeping him safe. I would gladly give my life to save Bear Man."

Bronco and Bear Dog enter the room as she is speaking. "You probably have given your life. Your tribe will hunt you down for what you've done. I'll do my best to protect you. But, my best may not be enough."

"Excuse me. I'll wait outside while you two talk." Patricia leaves the room quietly.

"Bear Man, I chose to do this. You owe me nothing. Please, do not feel responsible for what I've done. I don't know how War Eagle and my clan will react, but I don't want this settlement to suffer because of me."

"Issaqueena, I don't know exactly when I fell in love with you, but I can't imagine my life without you. Whatever happens, we'll face it together."

CHAPTER 32

Issaqueena doesn't have long to wait. The men of the village are repairing the covered passageway and constructing a strong gate to close it off. There will be no repeat of what happened yesterday.

Before the repair is completed, a fire starts near the opening of the passageway. The commotion draws Issaqueena outside. Several Cherokee braves hide behind the jail; their horses tied nearby. They capture Issaqueena and leave the village before anyone reacts.

"Where are you taking me?"

The brave replies, "War Eagle would like the pleasure of watching you die, and I'll do all I can to arrange it. I don't want War Eagle's wrath to fall on me."

"Bear Man will come for me, you know. You'll not make it to War Eagle. It's a long journey to Keowee."

The brave knows she is right. "War Eagle has entrusted me with this task, and I must do my best to return you to the camp alive. I do as I'm told."

"I'll never let you take me back. If Bear Man doesn't reach us, I'll kill myself. You know I mean what I say."

"I know," the brave's voice is very sad, "but we do what we have to do."

They have been riding for a long time when Issaqueena recognizes the area. She hears a waterfall nearby. She remembers going to the falls when she was a small child. She remembers playing in the pool beneath the falls.

"Could we stop for a short rest, please? The horses need water."

She watches the braves as they water the horses. She walks toward the waterfall. The braves call her name, and she begins to run. When she reaches the top of the falls, she dives into the cascading water.

Although she had told the braves she would kill herself before they reach the village, they weren't expecting this. They search the pool at the base of the falls. They check the weeds and grasses for signs of someone leaving the pond.

One brave turns to the others. "There was nothing we could do. War Eagle won't be pleased. He wanted to watch her die a slow death. She betrayed our tribe. Let's go. There is nothing more we can do."

Bronco walks up the creek to surprise the braves and take Issaqueena. He watches as they run toward the falls. He hears them call out as Issaqueena jumps. He waits as they search for her body.

He watches them leave without a body, and he knows Issaqueena has escaped.

When he reaches the base of the falls, he begins to call. "Issaqueena, where are you? They didn't have your body, so I know you are here. Answer me."

He watches as a vision of beauty walks through the falls with her arms outstretched for his embrace.

"I was sure you survived, but how did you manage this?"

"Remember when I told you I was not actually Cherokee." Bronco nods. "My Choctaw family came to these falls often. My friends and I found a small ledge behind the falls. We hid there when we played. The first time our parents searched for us, we sneaked up from behind and scared them. They were very angry with us. We didn't tell them where we hid. It was our secret."

"A very well kept secret that saved your life."

"Yes, and what shall I do with my life now?"

"We'll gather our things and travel to Charles Town. I attended school there. Many people have changed their names and blended into society. War Eagle and his braves won't find us there. I know some important people who will help us start over."

She sits in front of Bronco on the horse as they head toward 96. They follow the Keowee River toward the foothills; they talk about things they hope the future will bring.

They are distracted. Suddenly, the horse stumbles and falls to his knees. Issaqueena tumbles over the horse's head and rolls toward the lake below. Bronco jumps from the horse and races down the bank toward Issaqueena. She rolls into the water and disappears. As Bronco dives toward the water, he hears a loud clap of thunder and sees a flash of light that blinds him.

Something is terribly wrong. Bronco expects to be deep in the water, but there *is* no water. He lands face first on the red dirt parking lot of the J.C. Boozer Sports Complex.

Another clap of thunder and then a bolt of lightning… "No! No! This isn't Lake Issaqueena. I'm back in 96. The noise… the lights… it's the 4th of July Festival. I can't believe this has happened again."

"Bronco, where are you?" Michael was out of breath. "I'm running as fast as I can. Give me a break one time, will you?"

Bronco knocks the red dust off his buckskins. "Michael, did the fireworks go off? What happened here?"

"Nothing happened. That was just their warm-up explosion. It's not dark enough yet for them to begin the fireworks show."

"Michael, I think I'm going insane. I just had another one of those weird out-of-body adventures in 'Ole 96'. I'm going home right now and look up Issaqueena on the internet. I have to know what happened to her."

"Don't be silly, Bronc. The main fireworks display begins in about 20-30 minutes, and we haven't finished aggravating the girls, yet. Besides, you're not going to find a ride home now. Everyone is waiting for the fireworks display."

"I don't need a ride home. We're less than two miles from my house. I know this area like the back of my hand. I can run it in the dark."

"Yeah," Michael jokes, "and I guess Bear Dog will meet you halfway to protect you from bear attacks."

"As a matter of fact, yes. Bear Dog is Bear Man's constant companion, in the present and in the past."

Michael starts to laugh, "And just who is Bear Man?"

Michael hears a low growl behind him. He turns to see Bear Dog glaring at him in a very unfriendly fashion.

Bronco whispers, "I think it's safe for me to go home, now. I'll see you tomorrow."

Michael watches Bronco and Bear Dog jog down the dirt road that was a part of the original Cherokee Trail. The historic path is less than two tenths of a mile from the Manley's property.

Michael mumbles to himself. "If there is such a thing as warping back in time, Bronco lives in the right place."

Michael laughs and then yells at the top of his voice, "The British are coming! The British are coming! Run, Bronco. Run."